GHOSTS IN HORSESHOE CANYON

GHOSTS IN HORSESHOE CANYON

ROGER C. LUBECK

Ghosts in Horseshoe Canyon
Copyright © 2017 Roger C. Lubeck

Printing: 03/23/2021
LCCN: 2016920284
ISBN-10:1-944694-02-1
ISBN-13:978-1-944694-02-9
Pages 258

It Is What It Is Press
Publisher and Editor-in-Chief - Roger C. Lubeck
299 S. Foothill Blvd.
Cloverdale, California, 95425
www.iwiipress.wordpress.com
Copy editing: Joelle B. Burnette and Malena Eljumaily
Covers & interiors designed by: Roger C. Lubeck
Cover Photo: adapted from Zazzle, designer, Woodwalker
https://www.zazzle.com/anasazi+posters?si=250588791917759735
Photo of the Great Gallery from
https://commons.wikimedia.org/wiki/File:GreatGalleryPanel.jpg

Novels by Roger C. Lubeck

Night Raids, 2021

Buscadero, 2021

On the Half Shell, 2020

PT 777, 2020

Ghosts in Horseshoe Canyon, 2017.

Overland: Stage from El Paso, 2016.

Key West, a Robert Cederberg novel, 2015.

Port Royal, a Robert Cederberg novel, 2013.

Captiva, a Robert Cederberg novel, 2012.

Bullseye, a Robert Cederberg novel, 2011.

To the Western Border: A Fantasy Adventure, 2011.

DEDICATION

To Nette for her support and wisdom.

TABLE OF CONTENT

INTRODUCTION[1]

HORSESHOE CANYON

Horseshoe Canyon is west of Moab and East of Hanksville, Utah in Wayne County. Horseshoe Canyon is part of Canyonlands National Park. It is located west-northwest of the main park. Evidence of human activity dates back to 7000-9000 B.C., "when Paleo-Indians hunted large mammals such as mastodons and mammoths." Horseshoe Canyon contains rock art made by hunter-gatherers predating the Fremont culture and the Ancestral Puebloans. Originally called Barrier Canyon, Horseshoe's artifacts, dwellings, pictographs, and murals are some of the oldest in America. It is believed that the images depicting horses date from after 1540 AD; after the Spanish re-introduced horses to America.

WAYNE COUNTY

Wayne County was established in 1892 and named after a county in Tennessee. The county is 2,466 square miles and has a population of 2,778 or one person per square mile. The county is managed and policed by the sheriff and county government located in the town of Loa on the western border of the country. Part of Canyonlands and all of Horseshoe Canyon are in Wayne County, Utah.

CANYONLANDS

"Canyonlands National Park is a U.S. National Park located in southeastern Utah near the town of Moab. The park occupies

---

[1] Portions of this material in quotes were taken from Wikipedia.

527,497 square miles. It is managed and policed by the National Park Service. Legislation creating the park was signed into law on September 12, 1964. The park is divided into four districts: The Island in the Sky, the Needles, the Maze, and the combined rivers—the Green and Colorado.

The area was once home to the Ancestral Puebloans, of which many traces can be found. Although the items and tools they used have been largely taken away by looters, some of their stone and mud dwellings are well-preserved. The Ancestral Puebloans also left traces in the form of petroglyphs, most notably on the so-called Newspaper Rock near the Visitor Center at the entrance of this district. The Chocolate Drops buttes above the Maze. The Maze district is one of the most remote and inaccessible areas of the United States."

NAVAJO NATION

"The Navajo Nation (Navajo: Naabeehó Bináhásdzo) is a semi-autonomous Native American territory covering 27,425 square miles, occupying portions of northeastern Arizona, southeastern Utah, and northwestern New Mexico in the United States. This is the largest land area retained by a US tribe and is managed via agreements with the United States Congress as a sovereign Native American nation. The Navajo Nation has a government that includes a legislative house, an executive office, and a judicial system. The executive system manages a large law enforcement and social services apparatus, health services, Diné College, and other local educational trusts. The tribal police work in conjunction with local sheriffs and police departments."

HOLY GHOST

"The Holy Ghost or Earth God, door keeper to the 5th World of the Hopi and the Keeper of Fire, and Master of the Fourth World or Masauwv or Skeleton Man, the Spirit of Death surrounded by helpers. This display is believed to be a onetime ceremony, one perhaps marking the doorway to the underworld or the Sipapu of all Life! Also, an entrance to both Heaven and Hell."

https://southwestphotojournal.com/2013/07

GHOSTS IN
HORSESHOE CANYON

CHAPTER 1 - 5,000 BCE

 Sister-son lay at the base of a cottonwood tree, his lance at the ready. Mud and dung coated his body, making him a feast for the biting black flies, but his scent would not betray his presence to the herd. His father, Eagle Claw, and two uncles lay in the tall grass close to a female woolly mammoth.

Eagle Claw and a group of the clan's best hunters had been away from the village for many suns. The men had traveled far into the mountains before seeing the first woolly. Without meat for the winter, the clan would have to find a new place to live; one farther from the canyons and closer to the herds.

Sister-son admired his father as much as he feared him. Eagle Claws' hogan had many skulls, including a tiger he killed when he was still a boy; it also had the skulls of enemies killed in battle, and a few from clan members who had challenged Eagle Claw during a hunt.

Eagle Claw expected much from his hunters and more from his sons. Once when they were hunting alone, Sister-son stood to get a better view of the quick-horn they were hunting. The beast saw Sister-son and ran before his father could sling his lance. Sister-son knew he deserved a beating, but he could not walk for days. He hated to imagine what his father would do to anyone who made a mistake today. Even the smallest misstep on a hunt like this might cost the people ample food over the cold time.

1

The hunters encircled a large female that stayed back with a calf. The baby stopped to eat the tender reeds along the creek. Soon the mother and calf would be too far back for the bulls to protect. The calf moved up the creek, eating as it walked. The mother stopped to raise its long snout and sniff the air.

Giant beasts came down to the river and creeks during the hot time to drink and eat the tall grass and tender shoots along the river. The woollies like to wade into the deep water and get their entire bodies wet. They would drink water with their nose and then spray it at one another.

On his first hunt, Sister-son was too young to stand with the men in the circle of hunters. Instead, he watched from a tree. The herd had more calves than he had fingers and toes. Killing a calf was a simple task. Sister-son knew he could kill the baby with his lance and a club. The adults were different. It took at least ten hunters working together to bring down an adult. The males were the height of three men and four men long. Underneath the long coat of hair, a second, thicker layer of short hair and a layer fat beneath blocked their lances. For such a large creature, a woolly could move fast; faster than Sister-son's uncle, Chase-the-wind. For the hunters, the woolly's size and long tusks made an adult a worthy adversary.

Sister-son put his head down and waited. The circle of men and boys held their breaths as the cow smelled the air, her small eyes adding little to her detection of danger. A trumpet call from the calf made the cow return.

The cow used her tusks to push the hungry calf back to the herd. Unable to get the calf to hurry, she trumpeted to the trailing male. Eagle Claw signaled to attack. Sister-son and three other boys ran at the calf. When his lance pierced the baby's flesh, Sister-son experienced a deep sadness. *Was his hunger more important than this helpless calf's life*, he thought. Even as he and the others clubbed the beast to death, he wondered if the spirits looked on his actions and smiled. Sister-son vowed, once home, he would remember his first hunt with a painting on the great wall.

~*~

Eagle Claw placed stones in a circle around a pyre of wood and the fire keeper lit the stack. Sister-son used his stone knife and scraper to cut the hair and fat away from the calf's leg meat. They would cook a leg in the fire and then smoke the rest. The men would eat the beast's heart and liver tonight as a sign of respect for the giant. A group of boys, including Sister-son, would take the meat back to the village while the hunters continued to hunt. The trip back would take several suns. Sister-son wanted to remain with the men, with his father and uncles, but he also wanted to work on the wall painting with his grandfather.

~*~

Sister-son stood at the base of a wall ladder, holding it steady for Red Feet, his grandfather, and the tribe's wise man. The old man carried a clay bowl of red paint up the ladder. He was working on a wall drawing depicting the recent hunt in which hunters with lances were chasing a herd of quick horns. Sister-son watched the old man apply the red mixture to the wall. He used a skin scraper to shape the

3

flow of the wet red mud as it slid down the stone face. He tried to paint the woolly and her calf, but his old hands never seemed to get the beast looking right.

Red Feet painted on a long wall in a canyon up from the river. He said the place was holy. A place for the spirits from beyond. He used a mixture of charcoal from the fire, red clay, and animal fat to make pictures of the hunters and the animals they hunted. At the far end of the wall, he painted pictures of the dead and the great spirit. These images were larger and had no arms or legs.

"Where are their legs and feet, grandfather?" Sister-son asked.

"These are the ancients. The spirits who came before. They float on the wind. They need no legs to carry them."

"What about arms? Where are their arms?"

"If they had arms, they would try to interfere with the lives of the people. The spirits come to us to guide our thoughts. They come in our sleep, in our dreams. They have no legs or arms because death binds them."

"Is that the real reason? The other wall painters draw legs and arms, even hands and fingers, but you do not."

"I paint what I see; what I feel. My ancestors have no legs or arms. They are wrapped in the blanket they were buried in; I paint no more and no less. When you are older, you can paint what you see what you feel. Until then, get me more paint."

Sister-son walked to a group of boulders just beyond the wall. Toe holes served as steps to the top. A crack led to a small cave used by his grandfather to make and store paint. His grandfather had several caves where he kept pots of paint. Pots of red clay and pots with pig fat filled the cave along with knives, scrapers, cutters, and other tools used by his grandfather. Best of all were the lances and bow and arrows made by Sister-son's father. Eagle Claw made the best lances. Someday, when Sister-son was the tribes' wise man, he would paint his own great hunt on a canyon wall. Until then he had his own place to store his tools. A place high on the wall.

Wallace Fremont believed he was descended from the ancient people who lived along the Fremont River in southern Utah; the Fremont Culture People. Walt liked to tell people he was related to John Charles Frémont, the American military officer and explorer who led four expeditions into the west and earned the name, *The Pathfinder*. Walt's great grandfather emigrated from Holland and adopted the name of the town in Utah—Fremont—where he worked as a farm hand. His father and mother were both born in Fremont and became devoted members of The Church of Jesus Christ of Latter-day Saints (LDS). His father grew up on a farm and later worked for the railroad. Walt's mother died of cancer when Walt was sixteen. While she was alive, she made sure Walt attended primary and Sunday School.

Walt never openly rebelled, but he didn't fit in with the other boys. Walt told one of his Sunday School teachers that his mother's grandmother was an Apache; a claim refuted by the church and by local tribe members.

In junior high, Walt became active in the Boy Scouts. He learned to camp and survive in the waterless canyons. Riding came easily for Walt, and with the help of a bishop, he learned to shoot and hunt. He was a good hunter if a poor student in school. The one thing that captured Walt's interest was the practices and crafts of the ancient people. Walt learned how to flake stone to make stone tools and weapons. He even made ladders like those used in the pueblo. Sometimes on his visits to the canyons, he would dress like an Apache or Navajo from the time before the settlers when the native people ruled the west. He'd ride into the Maze wearing only a loincloth and a pair of calf-high deer-leather moccasins.

Walt collected pot shards and arrowheads as a boy. Occasionally he would find a whole pot. In high school, Walt came to realize he had a valuable, but illegal, collection of artifacts.

Walt worked as a janitor during his last year of high school. The job was easy, and Walt learned that if he was careful, he could steal from other students, the faculty, and the school. The principal, the bishop, and his father questioned Walt on more than one occasion, but he seemed so innocent, they always let him go. Walt came to think of lying as acting. It was years before Walt learned the term sociopath and applied it to his ability to deceive others.

Walt had a few male friends and no female friends, even at church. His knowledge of women and sex came from locker room talk and two playboy magazines Walt found in his father's closet. When Walt's father was at work, Walt would look at the pictures of nude women and masturbate. He imagined his father did the same.

The bishop in Walt's ward advised him that the best way to find a wife was to go on a mission. Walt wasn't interested in being a missionary or going to some foreign country for two years. What he was interested in was a more immediate avenue to sex. On television, in one episode of the Three Stooges, the three boys pretended to be stone-age men. They clubbed their women over the head and dragged them off to a cave. It would be two years before Walt would club and rape his first woman.

On June 6, 2010, a Sunday, Walt rode into Horseshoe Canyon before sunrise. He selected a spot to dig along a bend in the dry river bed a mile south of the Great Gallery. He'd found pot shards at the spot before. Walt had on shorts and a sweatshirt. He had long blond hair and a scraggly beard. To keep the dust out of his mouth, he had a bandana tied over his mouth like a cowboy.

On these expeditions, he always carried his folding Boy scout shovel, the type Army soldiers used in World War II; a shovel where the blade folded down, and the handle expanded.

"What are you doing?" someone shouted.

"What?" Walt asked.

A woman in her late twenties stood several feet away from Walt. She had on shorts, a T-shirt, and blue Nike running shoes. She had cropped blond hair under a baseball cap. She had a fanny pack around her waist with a water bottle hanging from her pack.

Walt stood up from the hole with the shovel in his right hand. A broken pot lay by the hole. The woman's sweat-stained shirt made her small breasts and swollen nipples stand out. Walt felt himself getting aroused.

"What did you ask?"

He gave her his dumb smile.

"I asked what you are doing. You can't take artifacts out of here. This area is protected."

"It's okay, I'm with the museum."

"What museum?"

"The Utah State Indian museum in Logan. We are doing a small dig in this area."

"Who is your boss and what is your name?"

"My boss? I don't understand. Why do you need all that information? If you want, I can show you my driver's license and my employee card from the museum." He reached into his back pocket and pulled out his wallet. He offered his wallet to her. When she reached for the wallet, he smashed the shovel blade on the side of her head. She dropped beside the hole.

Walt was so angry over her behavior and the situation, he nearly smashed her again with the shovel. However, Walt hated to destroy something so beautiful. Instead, he dragged her off into the cottonwoods where he bound her hands and arms with his belt. Walt cut away her T-shirt with his buck knife and used the shirt as a gag.

Walt had never touched a woman's breast. Her breasts were hot and sticky with sweat. Just touching her nipples made him cum, even before he could pull out his penis.

Walt cut away the woman's running shorts and panties. When he was hard again, he forced his penis into her unconscious body. The feeling of power and sexual release when he came again was like nothing he had ever experienced.

Exhausted, but flushed with pleasure, Walt rolled off the unconscious woman. He had to decide what to do. In her fanny pack, he found her wallet, with money and her driver's license. The woman lived in Heber. Her name was Cathy Medlow. Walt knew that he should kill her and bury the body. But he just couldn't kill her in cold blood.

He wanted to have sex again, but he needed a place to keep her. Since he didn't have a way to hide her, he made a risky decision. He wrote her a note. "I know where you live. I let you live. I didn't have to. I could have killed you. If you go to the police. I'll come to your home and rape and kill you."

He unbound her, took back his belt, and left her with her water bottle and torn shirt. His horse was less than a half mile south of his dig. He rode out of the canyon before the woman regained consciousness and read his note.

Cathy read the note twice. She believed if she talked to the police he would kill her. She was grateful to be alive, and although she ached from the rape, she was certain she would not get pregnant. The blow to her head left her with only a vague picture of the man and no memory of what followed her being hit on the head. In the end, she walked back to her car and drove to her motel. The event would be her secret; a lesson she would never forget or repeat.

Walt never forgot this first experience either. He learned two important lessons. First, he needed to hunt for pots and artifacts at night or during times when the chance of being seen by a park visitor was low. Second, he needed to find a place to hold his future victims.

CHAPTER 3 - Monday, June 6, 2016

Alice Sweetwater checked the bedroom and bathroom, one more time. The glowing number on the bedside clock read four fifteen. She would have liked to stay at the Hampton Inn or the new Hilton, but her grant from Utah State University only allowed fifty-two dollars a day for lodging at the Super-8 in Moab and twenty-five dollars a day for food. No one became an archeologist because of the money.

Alice carried her High Sierra hydration day pack, an extra jug of water, and a bag of energy bars and other snacks to the car. On the seat were her dark glasses, and a wide-brimmed straw cowboy hat. She would get a coffee to go from the hotel lobby. It was Monday morning. Alice planned to spend three days studying the ghost paintings in Horseshoe Canyon. On the television, a story about the Normandy invasion seventy-two years earlier caught her attention. D-Day. Alice loved studying about the past; at least the distant past. She wasn't as sure about current history.

In high school, Alice learned that Logan Canyon had once been under an ocean. On her trips to Mount Logan and Bear Lake, she collected fossilized seashells from the high mountain ridges. As an undergrad, she studied prehistoric native cultures. Alice had been a part of the team that saved artifacts from fifteen archeological sites during dam construction in Kanab. For her graduate thesis, she wanted to explore the gallery of wall art, the so-called Ghosts of Horseshoe Canyon. She hoped by spending two weeks studying the paintings on the gallery wall, she would discover some new insight into the ten-thousand-year-old paintings.

Archeologists believed the paintings predated the Fremont Culture. For thousands of years, nomadic hunter-gathers lived along the rivers and creeks in the canyons. People who hunted mastodons and woolly mammoths. Artifacts found in the canyons dated back to at least 6,000 years BC. The Fremont culture and Ancestral Puebloan also lived in the canyons at least until 1300 AD. The Great Gallery included both pictographs and petroglyphs. Most interesting of all were the triangle (tapered) figures, bodies without arms and legs, but with designs inside the figure. Researchers called this style, the Barrier Canyon style. Old-timers claimed Butch Cassidy hid out in Horseshoe Canyon at a spot called Robbers Roost.

In the 1900s, ranchers built stock trails into the canyon so livestock could water and feed. The National Park Service made Horseshoe Canyon a part of Canyonlands in 1971. This trip into the canyon would be Alice's fifth visit in two weeks; her first overnight stay on this trip. Alice and two other grad students, Bob Himmel from USU and Sara Glen from Weber had come to Moab to study the Great Gallery. The three met at a conference and discovered they shared a love for ancient rock art.

This trip was Alice's idea, part of her thesis. For Bob and Sara, the trip was a semi-vacation that allowed them the chance to sleep together again. After a week in Moab, it was clear; they had little interest in ancient art. After breakfast, they were leaving Alice on her own and driving to Las Vegas.

Alice passed the Canyonlands Information Center on her way to breakfast. During her week in Moab, she had gotten to know several park rangers. She was especially fond of one ranger, Willard Smith. He was tall and lean with beautiful blue eyes. Also, he was a Mormon. Alice had been raised as a Latter-day Saint, but her studies of native cultures made her question the teachings of the church. Talking with Ranger Smith, Alice realized she missed the comfort of the church, and she wanted a man in her life.

Alice stopped at the Information Center hoping to see Smith. Cal Hitchens greeted Alice at the front desk. Ranger Hitchens was close to retirement; on most days, he greeted visitors and answered questions about the parks. Once a week, he gave a tour of the Ghost Gallery in Horseshoe Canyon. Alice was twelve when she met Cal during a vacation with her parents. He was a true westerner who loved telling stories of the Native Americans and pioneers.

"Morning Alice," said Hitchens.

"Hey, Cal. Is Will around?"

"I think he's in the back offices. What are you up to?"

"Going to visit the ghosts later."

"Say hi for me."

"I will," she said, walking toward the back offices.

Alice found Ranger Smith going over a map of Capitol Reef. For an archeologist, Moab was at the center for dozens of prehistoric and early native sites. Canyonlands, Arches, Capitol Reef, and the

Canyon of the Ancients were all a short drive away. The same was true for a National Park Service ranger. The park system in the area affected four states.

Willard Smith was sitting at a large oak desk studying a map. A ranger's hat was on the desk beside him. His uniform looked laundered; his pants had a crease as did his shirt pocket. The morning light through an eastern window made his face seem pale even as his blue eyes shone.

"Miss Sweetwater. I didn't expect to see you today. I thought you'd be out at the Gallery."

Alice sat on the corner of the desk. "Later today. I'm having breakfast with my friends before they drive to Vegas. After that, I'm driving out to Horseshoe. I'm going to camp overnight and then go in early in the morning. I may stay over on Thursday and come back on Friday. I'm trying to save a little money on my grant."

"Who is going with you?"

"I'm going alone."

"This time of year, it is better to visit the park in a group."

"What do you mean?"

"The parks draw all types of people. Two years earlier, two men attacked a woman hiking alone."

"Where?"

"At Arches. We found her beaten and. . ."

"Raped?"

"Robbed and raped by two men."

"Why haven't I heard this story? Did you find the men?"

"The Moab police found one man right away. He is serving time in Draper."

"What about the other man?"

"That isn't so clear. The FBI searched for him, as did one of our Special Agents; she hunted him for a year, and so did the Indian tribal police."

"And?"

"I guess he is still on the loose. That's why I hate to see you hike alone."

"I have this." Alice lifted her jacket to reveal a Glock automatic.

"Firearms are not allowed in the parks. It is a rule."

"There is no rule about a can of Mace or a buck knife. I carry both."

"I guess you are more dangerous than the average tourist, but still, hiking with a group is safer."

"You could go with me."

"I would like to, but I have to go to Capitol Reef later today."

"How about tomorrow? You could meet me at the trailhead in the morning. I'll have donuts."

"It's possible I could meet you, but I won't know until late tonight." He pushed back from the desk.

"You can call me on my cellphone, or we can just meet at the trailhead," said Alice.

"If I can get away, I'll meet you by seven thirty. Will you wait?"

"Sure."

15

"Listen, even if I can't meet you, will you promise me to wait for a group of tourists so that you aren't alone going in?"

"Does it matter that much to you?"

"You matter that much," he said with a blush.

"That's sweet, and so are you."

"How about having dinner on Friday?" he asked.

"I'd like that."

Alice realized her attraction to a Mormon park ranger was foolish, but Smith was good looking, and he loved the land in the same way she did. She hoped Will would meet her at the trailhead tomorrow. She wasn't afraid, and she didn't mind being alone, rather she longed to share her love of ancient culture with someone special. Someone other than undergraduates taking an elective.

Bob and Sara were checking their e-mails when Alice arrived at the Red Rock Cafe and Net. Alice loved their muffins and breakfast bagels, plus they had great coffee and free Internet. The three friends spent two hours reading the newspapers and talking about the canyons and Vegas. Sara didn't want Alice going into the canyons alone. Neither did Bob, but he didn't go so far as to offer to cancel his plans for Vegas.

Breakfast was fun and a little depressing. Sara and Bob were in love and headed for Sin City. Alice didn't gamble, but she would have gone along if asked; she liked shopping and the restaurants. Unfortunately, Bob wanted to be alone with Sara.

In the parking lot, Sara and Alice promised to talk on the phone every night, and they agreed to meet in Moab for dinner on Saturday night. Alice didn't mention her dinner date with Ranger Smith, she was too superstitious.

Moab's central location made it ideal for visiting any of the parks, but it was not the closest town to Horseshoe Canyon. Alice drove north on Highway 191 to Crescent Junction, and then on US 70 to Green River where she stopped for gas and a bathroom break at the Gas-N-Go. She had stopped at the station three times before. Inside, a large, unkempt man with long blond hair and a three-day growth of beard watched her from the potato chip aisle. He had on a hunter's cap with flaps. He looked uncomfortably like the killer in the movie, *Fargo*.

Behind the counter, a smaller man wearing a shirt that said Gas-N-Go watched her as intently. When he took her credit card as payment for gas, a large iced-coffee, and a bag of popcorn, he said, "Another day in the canyon. Gonna be a hot drive."

"Have you ever driven on the road that goes to Horseshoe Canyon from here?" Alice asked. "It's County Road One Ten, I think."

"Gee, Miss Alice," he said, looking at her credit card, "I haven't been on that road in years. I usually go by way of Highway Twenty-four. How about you, ánaaí?" he said to the man in the hunter's cap.

Alice understood that ánaaí, was brother in the Diné language.

"What are you driving?" the man asked. He stepped forward and gave her a smile that was close to a leer.

"A ten-year-old Subaru. It's great for car camping, but. . ." She looked at the man. "Do I know you?" Alice asked.

"I don't think so."

"I can see you in some natural history museum. Do you collect Native American artifacts?"

"That's illegal, isn't it?"

"In certain places and certain items. Gee, you look familiar."

"One-ten is shorter," he said. "If I had a new jeep or an ATV, I might take One-ten, but it's a maze of unmarked dirt roads. If you had a breakdown, a pretty girl like you, I wouldn't like to think about what might happen." He smiled.

"Thanks, for the advice," she said. "Are you sure we don't know each other? My name is Alice Sweetwater."

"Here you are Miss Sweetwater." The attendant handed her back her credit card.

She took her card and left. In her mind, she pictured the blond man with short hair and ten years younger and fit. She was sure they knew each other as kids.

A hundred miles of paved highway preceded the turnoff for Horseshoe Canyon, and then another twenty miles on a dirt road. The trailhead consisted of an open parcel of land where people hiking to the Great Gallery parked for the day. The site had a vault toilet and a sign pointing to the trailhead. Visitors could camp on the land above the canyon, but not in the canyon.

Alice reached the trailhead a little after three in the afternoon. A pair of hikers were just going into the canyon even as a family of five was packing to leave. Alice planned to sleep in her car, just to be safe, but she set out her folding camp chair and laid a fire for later. Finished, she loaded her day pack, grabbed a camera, and set out for one of the lesser walls of primitive art. She would visit the Great Gallery and the Holy Ghost panel tomorrow with Ranger Smith. Today would be a short hike and some photos while there was light.

The small gallery was only a two-mile walk through the cottonwoods. The ancient artists had painted a hunt with deer-like animals running, and legless figures in among the herd. Alice took several hundred photos using a metal tape measure as a reference.

Finished for the day, she hiked back to her car where she found a pickup truck with a white camper top parked on the red clay just off the road. Beside the truck were a camp stove, two lawn chairs, and a four-person tent. Alice went to her car, dropped off her pack, and then used the toilet.

Once a fire was going, she made coffee on a gas camping stove and heated a can of Chef Boyardee ravioli. She loved the canned pasta as a kid and still did. For a while, she sat out by the fire watching the stars. The land was flat and empty except for scrub brush and rocks. The vast sky of stars and the isolation of the place made Alice feel cold and a little lost. She let the fire go out and then doused it with water. The owners of the pickup had not returned when she crawled into her sleeping bag and locked herself in the Subaru for the night.

Alice woke to the sound of coyotes howling in the distance. She reached for her Glock by her side. Even when their howls mixed together, they sounded lonely. The time on Alice's watch, read six-thirty-nine. Anxious to get started, she untangled herself from the sleeping bag. She needed to wash her face and brush her hair and teeth. She still hoped her ranger would show up.

In the car, she found the last donut from her snack bag. She divided it and ate half. Outside the car, she used the camp stove to boil water for coffee. She didn't want Smith seeing her drink coffee. There was no sign of activity by the camper and no one by the pickup, but the chairs and the tent were gone.

A man and a dog drove up in a station wagon. The dog raced ahead while the man gathered a day pack and walking stick out of the car. It was seven forty and no Ranger Smith.

"Excuse me," Alice called out to the man when he was back at his car. "Are you walking to the Gallery?"

"Yes."

"Mind if I walk along? My boyfriend wants me to hike with others."

"Where is your boyfriend?"

"He's late, but I'd like to get started."

"Well, you are welcome to join Ginger and me."

"Thanks, I'll get my gear, I'm Alice, by the way."

"I'm Fred, and this is Ginger." The man rubbed the head of an Irish Setter. "Do you have water?" He held up a gallon jug.

"Yes. I have a canteen and a water bag in my pack. Enough for two days if I need. By the way, I don't think they allow pets in this park."

"Ginger's special. She's a support dog. It's okay, I checked."

"Great, I'll let you lead."

Alice didn't believe the man about his dog. The dog didn't have one of those coats the relief dogs wear, and Alice had never seen a

Setter as a support dog. She guessed the man just liked breaking the rules, and anyway, Alice liked dogs. The three headed off toward the wall of native art, three and a half miles away.

CHAPTER 4 - Tuesday, June 7, 2016

"National Park Service."

"Thank God, there's something wrong. I need help."

"Where are you?"

"At the trailhead."

"Miss, you have to tell me where you are. Are you there? Miss, hello."

"Horseshoe. . ."

The caller disconnected. Grace Jenner, the dispatcher in the park service headquarters, called the number back but got no answer. She called the head ranger for the district. It took several minutes to find him. He had her issue an alert to all rangers after which, she contacted the park police and the special agent unit just in case. As the rangers checked in, she identified that Willard Smith and Cal Hitchens were the closest rangers to the Horseshoe Canyon trailhead. Hitchens was west of Green River and Smith was in Hanksville, just east of Capitol Reef. It was two twenty in the afternoon.

Cal Hitchens joined the U.S. Parks Service in 1987. He had one more year to reach his thirtieth and a gold-plated watch. He entered the National Park Service fresh out of the army. For a time, he loved living outdoors and caring for the environment. Now his knees hurt, so most days, he works the information desk or gives short tours. Cal was attending a meeting in Green River. The message said meet Ranger

Smith and investigate a call about trouble at the trailhead to Horseshoe Canyon. Nothing more, just meet and investigate.

Cal had been on a dozen calls like this. Most likely the problem was drunk campers or a family fight. Occasionally, a hiker needed rescuing, but rather than call for a rescue and pay the fee, the person in trouble called the park service and hoped for a kind-hearted ranger. Cal doubted there was an emergency, but once on the highway, he turned on his siren and pushed his Ford Explorer to ninety miles an hour. Fast driving was a sure cure for getting old.

On the access road, he slowed to a more reasonable speed. The road to the trailhead was flat and open—all red clay and sagebrush. The dirt road was double wide and well-marked with signs placed there by the Bureau of Land Management. Half way to the trailhead, the dust in the air indicated another vehicle had preceded him. Cal called the dispatcher to determine if Ranger Smith was ahead of him.

"He hasn't called in," said the dispatcher.

"Is his radio open?"

"We aren't sure."

"Keep trying."

When Cal reached the parking area, he pulled his service revolver from his holster and checked the chamber. He left the gun on the passenger seat. Parked off to the left side of the road was a Subaru. Across the road from the Subaru were a Dodge camper and a Honda station wagon. Ranger Smith was sitting on the sign leading to the trail. Cal parked the Explorer beside Ranger Smith's Jeep.

"What's up, Will?" Cal asked, getting out of his Explorer.

"Not sure. The cars are empty. You can't see into the camper, so I don't know."

"Should we run the plates?"

"It wouldn't hurt. I'm pretty sure that's Alice Sweetwater's Subaru. I talked to her yesterday. She said she was going to work at the Great Gallery this morning."

"I like that girl," said Cal.

"Let's check on the vehicles. You call in the plates. I'll check the camper."

Cal wrote the plate numbers on a notepad. Back in the Explorer, he called in, and gave the dispatcher the plate number for the wagon followed by the number of the Dodge. Just to be complete, he read the number for the Subaru. The dispatcher said she would be several minutes running the plates.

Smith walked around the camper looking in the driver's side window for a second time. He tried the driver's door.

"The windows have a black film on them."

"Try the back," Cal called.

Smith gave Cal a "duh" look.

He walked to the back of the camper and knocked. When no one answered, he tried the door. Smith had his hand on the butt of his pistol. At first, the door seemed locked. He tried again.

The back doors burst open without warning and forced Smith off his feet. Cal heard the explosion and watched the Mormon ranger's face turn from chiseled youthful beauty to bloody meat. Cal pushed open the driver's door with his revolver in hand, stepped out, aimed the pistol at the camper, and advanced. Smith was unmoving on the ground.

"You, inside. Throw out your weapon and come out." Cal had come too far to return to the Explorer. As he debated what to do, one of the back doors closed as the passenger door opened. Cal dove to the ground and fired a shot at the passenger door as he rolled to his right. He didn't see the figure exit the camper with the lance. He felt the head of the stone lance enter his back and sever his spine.

CHAPTER 5 - Wednesday, June 8, 2016

Mai Yázhí drew back her bedroom curtains. The blue-black morning sky meant it was still too early to run. She had been up half the night with her infant son, Ahote. He had his first cold, and Mai finally had to call her mother for advice and help.

Mai was a Special Agent for the National Park Service, stationed in Moab. Her territory included the Navajo Nation in the Four Corners of Utah, Colorado, New Mexico, and Arizona. She was a member of the Navajo tribe. She was raised in the Honághaahnii (One-walks-around) Clan. Ahote was her first child. She was raising him alone and working full time. Fortunately, she had her mother, sister Irene, and a dozen aunts ready to give advice and take care of Ahote when she was on a case.

The National Park Service Special Agents investigated murders and other major crimes occurring in the parks. A year earlier, Mai had been hunting a serial rapist. She was part of an FBI team working in two states. The man they called the Arches rapist had attacked four women in Arches National Park. The women were all hikers, hiking alone. He'd take his victim to an isolated spot, rape and beat her, and then leave her for dead. Three women had survived. Two described the man as small with dark features. One said he was blond. One thought he might be Native American because he wore some type of animal head on his head. One said it was a wolf. Another thought it was a coyote. The third woman was so traumatized, she never spoke. The FBI stopped looking eventually. Mai never gave up; she watched for new cases that fit the man's pattern. Now she was collecting information on a gang of artifact thieves; men who offered ancient arrowheads and pottery on the black and gray markets—relics that sold for thousands of dollars. So far, she didn't have a name or face, but some of the relics came from the Canyonlands and Horseshoe Canyon.

When the phone rang at eight after six, Mai was putting on her running shoes.

"Yázhí," she answered.

"We have a double murder and possible kidnapping in Horseshoe Canyon. This could be your boy. A car will pick you up in twenty minutes."

"Understood," said Yázhí. She would have liked to ask more questions, but every minute counted in a murder case. Mai woke her mother, grabbed her investigation kit, and retrieved her Glock from her gun locker. She put on a freshly laundered uniform. Instead of regular shoes, she pulled out a pair of hiking boots.

At the door, she kissed her son twice, and her mother and sister once each. They were her whole life.

~*~

Deputy Sheriff Hosteen "Hunter" Nalje (Hastiin Nalzheehii) picked up the call on the third ring.

"Hunter," he said. In the Navajo language, in Diné, Hosteen Nalje (or Hastiin Nalzheehii) meant "Man Hunter." Most people called him Hunter.

Nalje was sitting on his bed in his underwear. It was seven in the morning. Overnight it had rained. Soon the afternoon sun would dry out the rutted roads and turn the concrete into a pizza oven. Hunter had Wednesdays off. Wednesday for him consisted of doing laundry and working in his vegetable garden or riding. A corral and a horse barn surrounded Hunter's trailer. On mornings like this, after a rain, with the windows open and a slight breeze, the smell of hay, manure, and horse filled his senses. Not bad, exactly. A scent he had grown up with. But, a smell that made it difficult to date.

"Hunter?" the caller said.

Hunter yawned and rubbed a two-day-old beard.

"Is that you Chief?" Hunter asked. Sheriff Davenport never called. Hunter got out of bed. Like it or not, he would be working on his day off.

"Someone murdered two rangers in Horseshoe Canyon. Cal Hitchens and another man."

"Cal, murdered." Hunter looked in the mirror. *Who would kill Cal,* he wondered?

"You two were close?"

"Cal and I had beers on Sunday. He talked about retirement. How about the other ranger?"

"Willard Smith. He's stationed in Moab. He's a young guy, a member of the church."

"I don't understand. Who'd kill two park rangers?"

"Someone called and said something was wrong at Horseshoe Canyon. No name. Hitchens' called in three vehicle plates. A white

28

Dodge camper, now missing. The other two cars are still there. The park police have put out an APB on the white camper. The owner may be the person who killed the two officers. The Canyon is part of the National Park Service, but it is in Wayne County. I considered sending Glade Davis, but you are closer and my best investigator. I'd like you there if you can manage it. I'll understand if it is asking too much."

"I can be there in an hour." Hunter understood the Chief wasn't asking. It didn't matter.

"Ask for Special Agent Mai Yázhí. She's the park service's special investigator for the area."

"Small one. Is she Navajo?"

"I am assuming as least part. All I know is she's assigned to Moab from Salt Lake City."

"Is this a county case or federal?"

"Word is Yázhí is good, but so are you, and you're Navajo, too."

"Chief, where are the owners of those two cars?"

"The rangers are searching the park. Let's hope they are alive."

"You don't think they are."

"I'll wait for your report," said Davenport.

Hyrum Davenport had been elected as the Republican candidate for sheriff three terms in a row. In the last election, he ran unopposed. Hyrum was born and raised in Loa, Utah, the county seat of Wayne County. Davenport was much like the town. Loa had a population of just over six hundred people: 95 percent white and 98 percent Mormon. Sheriff Davenport knew very little about policing or crime investigation. He was an administrator and a good-old-boy community fundraiser. One day he would run for state office.

Hunter hung up the phone. He picked up a GLOCK 19 in a belt holster from a folding chair by his bed. Standing in the closet he pulled out a pair of jeans and a blue uniform shirt on hangers. From the foot of the bed, he stepped into a pair of Tony Lama boots. Looking in a mirror, he put on a Stetson Open Road; the same hat Sheriff Davenport had on his desk.

It took Hunter an hour to reach the trailhead. He parked his squad car across the road from a crime scene truck, five park ranger vehicles, a state trooper car, and an unmarked Ford truck. Hunter ran his fingers through his thick black hair before putting on his Stetson. Hunter loved his Stetson hats. He wore a felt Open Road in the winter and a straw version in summer. He considered wearing Stetson's shapeable Open Crown Fedora because the Fedora reminded him of the hats "Indians" wore in the John Wayne movies. However, Sheriff Davenport claimed Lyndon Johnson and the Texas Rangers wore the Open Road. Not a cowboy hat, he said, but clearly western. This was good enough for Hunter.

Hunter had very little to be vain about. Shorter than average, with a large nose, and thick eyebrows that dominated a rugged face, Hunter understood that he would never win a beauty contest. However, he had a sharp intellect and confidence in his own judgment.

Hunter recognized nearly everyone at the crime scene except a small Navajo woman wearing a park ranger hat that held in a mass of fine black hair. She was younger and prettier than he expected. She had on jeans, and a light, camel-colored bush jacket.

"Special Agent Yázhí," Hunter said. He stuck out his hand to shake. "Yá'át'ééh. I am Deputy Sheriff Nalje. I am Bit'ahnii (Folded Arms People) born for the Táchii'nii (The Red Running into Water Clan). My *cheii* is Tódích'íi'nii (Bitter Water Clan), and my *nálí* is Ta'neeszahnii (Tangle Clan). The sheriff sent me to see if I could help."

Among the Diné, the Navajo people, the first time you meet a new person your greeting included your name and then your mother's clan, father's clan, paternal grandfather's clan and maternal grandfather's clan. Among the people, a person's ancestry is important because it establishes your relationship to the other person. By tradition, men and women must marry outside of their immediate family clans.

"Yá'át'ééh," said Yázhí. "I am Special Agent Mai Yázhí. I am Honágháahnii (One-walks-around Clan) born for Tó'áhani (Near the water Clan). My *cheii* is Ts'ah yisk'idii (Sage Brush Hill Clan), and my *nálí* is Dzil tahini (Mountain Cove Clan). Do we know one another?"

"No. I just assumed you are the agent in charge."

"Are you really a hunter?"

"The men in my family have all been hunters. Some did little else."

"What about you?"

"My family name is Hastiin Nalzheehii."

"Man Hunter."

"During the week, my job is to hunt criminals. On Sunday, I do The New York Times crossword. Tell me about the case."

"The park rangers came in to investigate a disturbance. You can see where they parked." She took off her ranger hat and pointed to the two vehicles. "They called in three license plates. One is a missing Dodge camper. We assume someone in the camper shot Ranger Smith."

"What was the weapon?"

"Shotgun."

"What happened to Cal?"

"Hitchens was killed over here." Again, she used her hat to point to a marked spot on the red clay field. Hunter noticed how carefully she moved. She was exact and efficient.

"Shotgun?"

"The sheriff didn't tell you?"

"No."

"We found him with a lance in his back."

"An Indian lance? What tribe?" Hunter asked.

"Actually, the lance appears to be prehistoric. Made with a stone blade."

"How can that be?"

"You tell me. You are the one who does the crossword."

"What about the other cars?"

"The Subaru belongs to a grad student in archeology. She is here on some grant from USU to study the Great Gallery. They are searching for her right now. The wagon belongs to a local; one Fred

Gerber, age twenty-eight. I talked to his mother. She said Fred likes to hike the canyons. She said he had a dog with him. Ginger. He is a rock collector. He has one of those road side shops."

"What type of dog?"

"Irish Setter." Agent Yázhí pulled her long black hair into a ponytail and stuffed it back in her hat.

"Nice," said Hunter, looking at Yázhí.

"The dog or my hair?"

"Both, I guess," Hunter laughed. "What would you like me to do?"

"We need to let the crime scene people do their job. I plan to join the searchers at the bottom. Would you like to go along?"

"I am not really dressed for a hike." Hunter pointed to his Tony Lama boots.

"I don't plan to hike. I am going in on one of those." She pointed to two ATV four-wheelers on a trailer.

"It's going to be hard going in from here. The start of the trail is steep and narrow. Those are likely to damage some of the plant life. Disturb the Dino prints."

"There is a trail in from the south. We'll drive to the Hans Flat Park Station. They say we can go in without any damage. Are you game?"

"Let me get my rifle and a jacket."

"What about the boots?"

"I could go barefoot like when I was a kid, but I have a pair of Kélchí in the car."

"Moccasins?"

"I've taken up dancing in pow wows."

"Are you a singer?"

"I was kidding. I wear them riding my horse."

Visitors departing from the trailhead had to walk in and out. The hiking trail into the canyon was wide and flat in most spots. The beginning of the trail dropped over seven hundred feet down to the ancient river bed. Once the hikers reached the river bed, they had a decision, turn east and head to the Green River, or turn southwest toward the wall art. Those riding horses left from a different station in the park. Twenty miles west, off-road vehicles were allowed access from Hans Flat. The drivers of the four-wheelers were two of the park services' most experienced and knowledgeable officers, Ed Foster, and Chet Manwing.

Hunter climbed on the ATV behind Chet Manwing. Agent Yázhí put a two-gallon water jug in the ATV and climbed behind Ed Foster. Manwing pointed out landmarks along the way; he claimed he knew every dinosaur footprint and ancient artifact in the canyon.

"There's a Dino print," he called. Fossilized dinosaur prints were usually marked by a circle of stones. Visitors can look but not touch. The same went for pot shards and arrowheads.

Before driving to the "Gallery," Agent Yázhí set one of the water jugs in the shade of a cottonwood tree. Even though the canyon was called Water Canyon, there was no water for miles.

Watching Yázhí, Hunter was impressed with her practical carefulness. The temperature could reach over ninety in the shade.

Hikers needed to carry at least a gallon of water for the trip in and out of the Gallery. Hopefully, they would need less water riding on the ATVs, but Yázhí was a planner. She didn't take chances. Hunter liked that in a partner.

For the first five years of his life, Hunter lived in a hogan on a reservation near Navajo Mountain. The name *Navajo* comes from the Spanish. Among the Navajos, the people are called, Diné. Hunter's family lived with his mother's parents in a hogan. Their hogan was built for year-round living. Square-shaped, rather than round, with timber and stone walls packed with earth, the dwelling had a single door covered with a large handmade Navajo blanket. The door faced east to welcome the rising sun. Navajos believed this would bring wealth and fortune. In the winter, his mother moved the fire inside to warm the house.

Hunter's father and grandfathers raised sheep and farmed corn and squash. His mother started weaving as a girl. His grandfather built a second, smaller round hogan for the women to weave in. On the reservation, Hunter spent considerable time on a horse. He and his father and his uncles would ride into one of the canyons where they would hunt and fish. For Hunter, hunting and camping became a way of life until he was in high school. Hunter was one of thirty students to attend Navajo Mountain High School. For his first year, he rode his horse to school.

At school, Hunter loved sports, especially baseball and soccer. As a boy, he and his brothers and cousins had played stick ball. Hunter was only an average student, except for language. He had a good ear for language. In grade school, he spoke Diné and learned English and Spanish. In high school, English literature became his passion. He read Shakespeare and Joyce.

Hunter learned about the creation of the Diné people from stories told by his father and grandfathers. His grandfather on his father's side was a healer who told the stories in the Diné language. He sang at ceremonies. Hunter could still hear his grandfather singing for his sister's first laugh and her first step. Hunter's father had practiced the old ways before he fought in the first Gulf War. When he returned to the Nation, he drank. Before the war, his father told creation stories in the language of the Diné. After fighting the white man's war, when he told stories, they were in English. It was a sign of the times. Hunter enjoyed the stories of the five worlds and stories about First Man and First Woman, Changing Woman, and the Monsters.

Best of all, Hunter enjoyed the story of Naayéé'neizghání (Slayer of Monsters) and Tóbájíshchíní (Born for Water), the "Navajo Hero Twins." They were born of Changing Woman and for their father, the sun. He loved the story of how the boys visited their father and he gave them lightning arrows with which they killed the monsters that preyed on his people. Only later did Hunter understand the monsters were the children of the sun, and Slayer of Monsters and Born for Water were killing their own brothers and sisters.

In the Indian school, Hunter learned the other tribes had similar stories of sacred mountains and floods. Hunter came to realize, the children who spoke the Diné language and wore traditional dress were considered the poor children. Raising sheep meant that Hunter's family would always be poor. Being poor and the butt of jokes made Hunter so angry that he began to disavow his traditional upbringing.

Out of high school, he joined the Army. After basic training, a captain in the Military Police approached Hunter. He said Hunter would make an excellent Combat MP. After his basic MP training, Hunter did a tour in Afghanistan and Iraq. The Army sent Hunter to a special course at the Military Police School at Fort Leonard Wood, Missouri. His academic record there led to training through the Apprentice Criminal Investigation Division Special Agent course. Hunter proved to be a perfect student and a good cop.

When Hunter returned from service in Iraq, he returned to Navajo Mountain. His Uncle Joseph wanted him to take part in pow wows and learn to sing, but Hunter felt he no longer belonged. He spoke the language of the people, but he thought like a white man. No, that wasn't right, he thought like a cop. He had spent the last five years living primarily with white police officers. He shared their values their ambitiousness and competitiveness.

Hunter considered working for the tribal police or the National Park Service. Somehow, Sheriff Davenport had gotten word that Hunter was looking for police work. Hunter had a reputation for being dogged and getting results. Davenport contacted Hunter and invited him to interview for a job as a deputy sheriff in Wayne County.

In the interview, Davenport told Hunter he could never be elected for Sheriff of Wayne County because he was a Navajo, a non-Mormon, and a Democrat. However, the old sheriff added, he would be honored to have a hero and police officer like Hunter work in his department. He also acknowledged Hunter would be the only Native American criminal investigator in the county. To sweeten the deal, Davenport rented out a trailer he owned in Hanksville to Hunter, and he arranged for space in a horse barn where Hunter kept one of the mustangs Davenport had given him from his ranch.

Hunter's nearest neighbor in Hanksville, Kim Wheatley, maintained the horse barn and corral where Hunter kept his horse. Hunter called the painted pony Blackie, and he and Wheatley rode on weekends. Hunter would wear jeans and red moccasins and ride Blackie bareback, the way he rode as a kid.

~*~

It took half an hour to reach the canyon wall with the ancient art. Two hundred feet long and divided into two sections, the larger long section had over twenty-five large paintings. Archeologist estimated that these paintings could be ten thousand years old. The smaller section contained five figures. They were painted on a section where the wall had fallen away. Researchers speculated there were paintings on the original face when the wall collapsed. The figures on this wall were painted less than a thousand years earlier. Different times and different artists. South of the wall was a large group of boulders, and then another wall, this one unmarked. Why the ancients had painted one wall, but not the other, was another mystery.

Hunter chambered a round into his Winchester rifle before leaving the ATV. He carried the rifle over his left arm, just as had his ancestors. Agent Yázhí left her ATV and approached the sandstone wall.

"Have you been here before?" asked Agent Yázhí.

"Not since I was a kid."

"What do you think?" She touched the stone wall.

"About the case?"

"No, what do you think when you see these wall paintings?"

Hunter joined her at the wall. One of the larger figures seemed to stare at him. "I wonder, who were these people? How did they live in such a barren place? I remember coming here as a kid. I came with my grandfather. He said the ancient people painted these walls long before our people lived on the earth. He was a singer. He said the paintings came alive at night. He called this the 'Ghost wall.' At first, the paintings scared me. Those faces look like skulls, and where are their arms and legs?"

"My father claimed they are spirits watching over their people. He said this was a very spiritual place, like a church," Said Yázhí.

"Is that what you believe?"

"Christians decorated the windows and walls of their churches as a sign of their wealth. The ancient people painted on walls all over the world. I don't think they are the same," she said.

"What do you feel when you see something like this?" Hunter asked.

"Lonely and connected all at the same time." Agent Yázhí turned to hide her tears. Hunter wanted to say that he felt the same, but in fact, he felt very little. He was focused on finding the missing girl and catching the killers. Looking at the thousand-year-old paintings, he was thinking like a cop.

Ed Foster rode north to talk with the rangers searching on foot. Chet Manwing picked up a bullhorn from the supply basket at the back of the ATV. He would drive north toward Water Canyon.

"Alice Sweetwater," he called. "Fred Gerber." The names echoed off the painted walls. Nothing returned.

"Alice, Fred. We are with the park service. Call out if you can."

Manwing handed Hunter the bullhorn. Hunter called their names. Nothing. Hunter turned south and called again. He turned east and called. When he turned back west, he saw that Agent Yázhí had climbed the path up to the face of the Ghost Wall. Against all instructions, she had both hands on the wall as if she was taking energy from the paintings. Chet Manwing and Hunter exchanged a look but said nothing. These haunting symbols affected people differently.

Ed Foster returned. He said there were no recent signs of a woman, or a man and dog going north from the trailhead. Hunter and Foster left Agent Yázhí at the wall. They each searched the immediate area for any signs of Alice or Fred.

Hunter found the top to a container of yogurt. Chet found dog, rabbit, and coyote scat. Ed found nothing. Frustrated, the three men met back at the ATVs and waited for Mai Yázhí to leave the wall.

"I saw no signs, what about you," Yázhí asked the three.

"Nothing," said Foster. "We should work our way back."

"They are dead," said Chet Manwing.

"No, they are alive," said Yázhí.

"How can you know?" asked Chet Manwing.

"The walls told me."

 Mai took a moment to consider what clothes she would wear to her meeting with Deputy Nalje. She seldom wore her ranger uniform, and dresses even less. Her mother wore the traditional blue skirt and white blouse that women on the reservation wore. At home, Mai wore blue jeans and T-shirts. Before she married, she wore fashionable pants and sheer blouses, with a jacket to hide her pistol. She even wore makeup. That seemed like another time.

Hosteen Nalje had changed her attitude about dating. He might be on the short and homely side, but he wore nice clothes, he loved the outdoors and horses, and most important of all, his parents and grandparents were from different tribes.

Mai's mother, Janet, had a hard time accepting Mai's Hopi husband into her family. Mai would have to find a Navajo man from a different clan if she wanted to marry again. Even with over one hundred clans, most people belonged to one of the four original clans. Nalje was Bit'ahnii, and Mai was Honághááhnii. Fortunately, their fathers and grandparents were all from different clans. Nalje fit the bill, and as he said, he did the New York Times, too. Mai picked out a dark lipstick. She applied a thin line of lipstick and then gloss. In the mirror, she looked like a different person.

Mai's mother Janet was waiting for her at the door. Ahote was asleep in her arms. "What are his clans?"

"I told you, Folded Arms People, the Red Running into Water Clan, Bitter Water Clan, and Tangle Clan."

"Bitter Water Clan. Is he tall and good looking?"

"No, he's small and a bit homely. And, he seems vain. He wears expensive white man's clothes. Yet—"

"Yet?"

"He is like the Gray Wolf. There is a strength to him and determination. He is called Hunter for a reason. I am hoping he will find the girl."

"Changing woman created Gray Wolf to protect the Bitter Water Clan. Your Hunter is part Bitter Water. People say the Bitter Water Clan and One Walks Around Clan produce strong children."

"Don't be silly. We are just partners on a case. He's a cop."

"Still, he is suitable and available."

"It's just lunch at Milt's."

"Ahote needs a father."

"He had a father," said Mai, trying not to raise her voice.

"A Hopi!"

"He died for his country."

"Ahote needs a Navajo father. A protector."

"I'm going. I'll see you for dinner."

~*~

Hunter had a meeting scheduled with Sheriff Davenport at eight in the morning in Loa. He left Hanksville at six thirty. Hunter liked the morning. Some days, he'd ride Blackie, his painted Indian pony, in the hills outside of Hanksville. Away from the trailers, the derelicts and abandoned cars, and the piles of used tires and washing machines that surround most homes in Hanksville, Hunter became his namesake, a hunter. He'd ride Blackie bareback with just a blanket for a saddle. Hunter had never mastered the bow and arrow, but he could use a sling. Sometimes he and Blackie would ride into a prairie dog town or stumble across a rabbit, and Hunter would sling a stone the way his mother taught him. Now, instead of a sling, he carried a military-style Glock automatic.

The sheriff's office was in the county courthouse in Loa. Hunter used a computer he shared with four others to finished his summary of the search in Horseshoe Canyon. Most police officers spend half their careers filling out forms and reports. At the far-western end of the county, the town of Loa had fewer than six hundred residents. Though not much bigger than the other nearby towns, Loa had more businesses because of its being the county seat. The next largest town, Torrey, was the jumping off point for people visiting Capitol Reef. It had more gas stations and motels, but fewer people.

Hunter lived in Hanksville, sixty miles from the office. Typically, his job comprised patrolling the highway between Hanksville and Torrey and giving out traffic tickets. If there was a significant crime, Hunter would investigate the crime with sixty-year-old Glade Davis. Twice a week, Hunter spent time in the Loa office with Sheriff Davenport. Once a month, he had the front desk and jail detail.

In his late fifties, Sheriff Davenport had thinning gray hair cut in a military style. Davenport had a politician's smile and handshake. He was at one time, the bishop of his ward. He claimed he was sheriff because the pay was the same as the mayor with fewer problems. Davenport wasn't a career policeman, which was why he had men like Hunter and Glade Davis. In the next election cycle, he planned to run for state representative.

Hunter reported that the search was continuing in the canyon because Special Agent Yázhí said Alice Sweetwater was alive. Hunter didn't mention a meeting with Yázhí later in the morning for fear the sheriff would tell him to stay in Loa and let the Feds and the state police search for the white camper.

The Division of Motor Vehicles showed one Wallace Fremont, a resident of Lyman, Utah, owned the camper. Deputy Sheriff Blake Young reported no camper and no sign of Fremont at his trailer in Lyman. The sheriff arranged for a daily check and told the other deputies to call Hunter as soon as Fremont returned home.

Hunter printed three copies of the finished report, one for the sheriff, one for his file, and one for Special Agent Yázhí. He put the report in a manila envelope along with his business card. Before leaving for Moab, he checked with the desk officer. No one had seen Walt Fremont or the white camper.

~*~

Agent Yázhí said she lived near the park headquarters in Moab. For unexplained reasons, she said she wanted to meet outside of her office, perhaps for lunch. In picking a place to meet, Hunter considered the Moab Diner. A hangout for law enforcement, the diner served breakfast all day. Yázhí said she wanted a place away from city hall. Hunter suggested Milt's on Locust and Fourth. A classic burger and shakes place with picnic tables on the side, Milt's was the oldest restaurant in Moab.

For over a year, Hunter had been trying to be a vegetarian. He grew up eating squash and beans with a little lamb or venison meat during hunting season. Now, when Hunter killed a deer, he gave most of the meat to his relatives on the reservation. Not eating steaks wasn't much of a challenge. Bacon was harder. The one food he couldn't give up was burgers. He loved a good burger. It could be a hamburger or a turkey burger, even a tuna burger. He even had a tofu burger once. So long as it was grilled and on a bun.

The front of Milt's had a painted sign that read, "Stop and Eat. Good Food since 1954." According to the restaurant's menu, Milt had served in the Pacific during World War II. After the service, Milt and his wife, Audrey, lived in Iowa where Milt was a short-order cook. On a camping trip with a friend, Milt spent the night on the Colorado River in Moab. The next day he called Audrey and told her to pack. They moved to Moab and started their diner in 1954. Originally, the diner was on Main Street. Then Main Street moved.

Milt's was a classic diner with an open grill and kitchen, vinyl-topped stools, and a Formica counter. The restaurant has had four owners since Milt and Audrey, but little has changed. The number one item on the menu is a chili-cheeseburger, fries, and a milkshake.

Inside, the counter stools were all taken by working men, mostly truckers in jeans and T-shirts. Each man with a different ball cap with the name of his freight company. Outside under the large sycamore tree, there were picnic tables and round bistro tables.

Agent Yázhí was sitting at a round table drinking a milkshake when Hunter arrived. She had on jeans, a flannel shirt, and a down vest. If she had a weapon, it wasn't obvious. Today she had replaced her ranger hat with a ball cap.

"Are you cold?" Hunter asked, pointing to Yázhí's vest. He took off his Stetson and fanned his face. A temperature gauge on a nearby tree read "eighty-nine."

"No, the vest is to cover my gun."

"Did you order already?"

"Just a shake."

"What can I get you?" Hunter asked.

"How about a chili-cheeseburger and fries?"

"Sounds good, I'll be right back. Here is my report."

He handed her a manila envelope. She was still reading the report when he returned with food.

"This is very thorough. I like the way you write. The report is organized. You set out the facts in a clear manner." She took a moment to put ketchup on her burger and fries.

"What did you get?"

"A veggie burger and a peanut butter malt."

"Are you a vegetarian?"

"I'm not a vegan if that's what you mean, but I try to eat healthy when I can." Hunter didn't like being criticized for his habits.

"Why didn't you include the background information on Fremont?"

"I didn't have any. What do you know?"

"He is a piece of work. Married and estranged."

"Not divorced?"

"No, she's Mormon."

"Who isn't?" He smiled at his own humor until he saw her frown.

"I'm sorry, are you LDS?"

"No, but I have family members who are Mormons. Are you?"

"I was taught in the old ways. I mentioned my grandfather on my father's side was a singer. I want to believe in the old ways. My mom still lives on the res. She lives in a hogan."

"I wish I could. I don't believe in anything. Except that evil exists."

"Tell me about Walt Fremont."

"He was arrested on spouse abuse but released. He owns at least four guns, including a Remington hunting rifle and a shotgun. A neighbor claimed Fremont killed his dog, but the police found no evidence, except that someone had broken the dog's neck."

"What does he do for a living?"

"He's on disability. He was injured in an incident at the museum where he worked as a janitor. A doc said his back was injured and he can't work, so he gets twice his monthly pay for life."

"What about his wife?"

"We did a phone interview. She said he goes off for weeks at a time. She thinks he is in Vegas. I talked to her on the phone. She seemed unusual."

"Do you like him for this?"

"I want to talk to him. We have nothing else.".

"What about the lance?"

"I sent it to our C-I-D in Provo. They are going to consult with an artifacts expert at a museum in Salt Lake. There are people today who know how to make a stone spearhead. The harder part is the wooden shaft. It should be carbon dated. My guess is it is new wood, but a great copy."

"Could it be real? Maybe stolen from a collection or a museum?"

"I'll put someone on that idea," said Mai.

"What about the FBI? Are they involved yet?"

She picked up her malt and drank some. "They'll send someone if I ask," she said, with a frown.

"Is that what you want?"

"No, I want to catch the bastard who killed Smith and Hitchens."

"What about Alice?"

"When we catch Walt, we'll find Alice. He has her. I'm sure of it. She's a trophy."

"She's a witness. If I were him, I'd dump her somewhere. We know his camper was there, but that doesn't mean he was. It's only circumstantial. We'd need more to connect him. We need Alice."

"Or Fred Gerber."

"I keep forgetting about him. He doesn't fit. We should talk to his mother."

"I don't have the time. I need to focus on Walt. Perhaps we

should split up. You follow up on Fred and Alice, and I'll go after Walt."

"Is that what you want?" Hunter asked.

"Honestly, I want another chocolate shake." She holds out her glass. He laughed and gots up to get her a shake.

"I like you," she said. "I think we should work this case together."

"I like you, too. After lunch, we should go look at Walt's trailer and talk to his wife."

"Get the shake to go."

He went into the diner.

Yázhí was on her cellphone when Hunter returned with an iced tea for himself and a milkshake for her. She signaled him to sit. "Leave everything as it is," she said into the phone, "we will be there in two-and-a-half hours. Have the ATV meet us at Hans Flat."

"What is it," he asked when she finished the call.

"They found the dog. The Irish Setter."

"Where?"

"Near the Great Gallery."

"How did we miss it?"

"Someone buried it. I think we need to go look for ourselves."

"There's something else isn't there?"

"The dog's neck was broken. Can we go in your truck? They will have a pair of ATV waiting at Hans Flat."

"I'll need to change out of these clothes." He pointed to his expensive Tony Lama boots. "I usually have hiking boots or sneakers in the car. But, not this time."

"What size are your shoes?"

"Size?"

"Shoe Size."

"I wear a size nine, Why?"

"We can stop at the Visitors Center and get you a pair of genuine Navajo moccasins, made in China."

"I'll wear these."

~*~

They reached the crime scene team in the late afternoon. The dog had been buried in the sand near a cottonwood tree. The dead Irish Setter's nose stuck out of a black body bag. A park ranger stood over the bag. Two rangers were walking in circles using metal detectors. Two more used metal probes to search for other bodies. Agent Yázhí approached a ranger standing by the bag.

"Ranger Tsinnie, who found the dog?"

"I did. Jason and I."

"How?" Hunter asked.

"We saw the buzzards." He pointed to the vultures circling overhead.

"How deep was the grave?" Yázhí asked.

"He used a shovel," Ranger Tsinnie said.

"How can you tell?" Yázhí asked.

"I tried to dig with my hands. It's possible, but slow work."

50

"No one walks into this canyon carrying a shovel," said Yázhí.

"How about a folding Army shovel," said Hunter,

"Or a Boy scout shovel," said Jason.

"Sure, a camping shovel," said Hunter.

"Why kill the dog?" asked Yázhí, to no one.

"Maybe he had a history. Maybe Gerber and Fremont knew each other." said Hunter.

"We should talk to Gerber's mother," said Yázhí. "He lives in Green River."

"We should have stopped before we came here."

"I can have someone from Moab check on Gerber. I think we should stay here. There could be more bodies."

"The boy may be here. I'm guessing he is, but the girl isn't," said Hunter.

"How can you be sure?" asked the ranger.

"The killer waited for the girl. Down here by the wall. He didn't expect the dog or the man. Only the girl." Hunter looked at the Great Gallery.

"It's possible he didn't expect anyone. He was here digging for artifacts," said Hunter. "He's found a cache. That's where the lance came from. There's a burial site here. The girl surprised him, but she wasn't alone. He can't let her live, so he figures it is easier to walk her to his camper. Somewhere he meets the man and the dog and kills them."

"I don't see it," said Yázhí. "It seems thin."

"I know, but it explains why he shot Ranger Smith," said Hunter.

"Because he had Alice in the camper," said Yázhí.

"And, Smith knew Alice."

"And, Wallace Fremont knew Smith."

"Who is this guy, Wallace Fremont?" Ranger Tsinnie asked.

"I think he's our killer," said Agent Yázhí. "Let's go to Lyman."

"It's too late. It would be after nine."

"Alice has been missing for two days. She doesn't have the time for us to go back and forth to Moab. We should stay in Hanksville and go in the morning, first thing. After that, we would have most of the day to follow any leads."

"What's in Hanksville?"

"It's where I live. I have an extra bedroom."

"I have to make a few calls, first. Is there a place we can eat?"

"I know just the place," he said, smiling.

On the drive to Hanksville, Agent Yázhí and Deputy Nalje became Mai and Hunter. They talked about growing up. Mai mentioned again that her Navajo nickname was At'eed Mai, or bright flower. Hunter admitted as a boy, he was called Kilchii (Red Boy), which became Hunter in school.

"Does anyone still call you Red Boy?"

"My mother does. I was fussy as a baby. I guess I cried all the time. The day I was named, I was red from crying."

"I have to say; you don't really seem like a Hunter to me. Where did the Hunter come from?"

"In high school, I liked to hunt. My father and I hunted every weekend. Dad started calling me Ashkii Nalje, Boy-Hunter. Eventually, folks called me Hunter at school, Hosteen Nalje in town, and Hastiin Nalzheehii at home. But, the army changed everything. When I joined the Military Police, my brother started calling me Silaigo, Policeman. I hated that."

"Personally, I like Nalzheehii. Can I call you Hunter?"

"If I can call you Mai."

"I'd like that."

Hunter called the sheriff's office. "Agent Yázhí and I are going to Lyman in the morning to check out Fremont's trailer," Hunter told Deputy Blake Young. "See if the sheriff can get me a warrant. I'll be at Fremont's trailer by eight in the morning. You can bring the warrant to me."

"What are you doing now?"

"I'm going home."

Hanksville was twenty miles west of the canyon road on Utah Highway 24. Settled in the 1880s and named after Mormon pioneer Ebenezer Hanks, the town consisted of a gas station, a scattering of homes and trailers, an ancient grist mill, and a pioneer LDS church building across from a newer ward building and a new church. The town is known for uranium and gold booms, and for the Mars Desert Research Station located outside of town. The welcome sign reads "Established 1882, population two hundred and nineteen, give or take a jackass or two." It is said Butch Cassidy came to Hanksville for supplies.

Hunter's yard and trailer were clear evidence of Hunter's personality. Free of any debris or clutter, the yard was fenced with a patch of cut grass on the right side of the yard. Hunter had planted roses in the front. He liked the smell and the beauty of new growth and color month after month. On the left side of the trailer was a twenty-five-foot by fifty-foot vegetable garden. Visible were lettuce, tomatoes, squash, and corn.

"Is this yours?" Mai asked, pointing to the garden.

"I do the watering. My neighbor and I share the gardening work and the vegetables."

The inside of the trailer matched the yard. It was neat, clean, and orderly. Most trailers were filled with junk, junk furniture, and the owner's personal collection of stuff. Hunter's kitchen was small with a sink free of dishes. The living room had two La-Z-Boy chairs, a reading lamp, and a TV. Hunter showed Mai the spare bedroom. It had a twin bed, chair, dresser, and a clock radio.

"I have to make some space in the bathroom. Would you like to change? I have shorts and a T-shirt or sweats you could probably wear. That way you'd have the clothes you're wearing for tomorrow."

"Do you have a washer and dryer?"

"I do, although they are the size of a suitcase."

"Should I keep these clothes on for dinner?"

"No, the place we are going to allows shorts and T-shirts."

"Good, then I'll change out of these."

It had been months since Hunter had been with a woman, let alone had a woman in his trailer. He picked out several shorts and T-shirts and a pair of sweats.

He knocked on the bedroom door. "The washer and dryer are next to the bathroom. There's soap in a box. I put clothes for you by the door. I'll be out back," he said.

~*~

Mai took her time changing. It felt good to lie on the bed and relax, knowing her mother was taking care of everything at home. After putting her clothes in the washing machine, she used the bathroom and then peeked into Hunter's bedroom. It was messier than the rest of the trailer but orderly.

Outside Hunter was standing by a Weber Kettle charcoal grill. He was squirting lighter fluid on already-flaming charcoal. Beside the grill was a table with a bowl and a plate of buns. Next to the grill, was a picnic table. At the back of the yard, a half dozen chairs and stumps formed a horseshoe around a fire pit.

"What is this, Hunter's Grill?"

"Would you like an iced tea or a beer with your burger?"

"Is there wine?"

"I think so. I can't guarantee the quality."

"Any port in a storm."

"Was that a joke? A double entendre?"

"No just a phrase I use. A double entendre. You really do crosswords."

"I'll get you a glass. Do you want white wine or white wine?"

"White is good. What can I do?"

"Pick lettuce for a salad. It is in the side garden. There are several types. Also, there is cabbage. Do you need me to show you which is which?" He handed her the bowl.

"I'm a detective. I'll be right back."

Hunter added milk-soaked bread, egg, and cut up mushrooms and onions to the meat. When this was mixed, he folded in venison meat. He formed two patties each and set them aside while Mai cut tomatoes and cucumber. Hunter liked cooking on the grill, and more and more, he liked being with Mai.

"This burger is delicious," said Mai. "Is there more wine?"

"I'll get the bottle."

"No just a glass. Is there dessert?"

"I think I have ice cream or cookies."

"No donuts?"

"I can make fry bread."

"Get me some more wine and let's go watch the sunset." Mai pointed to the sun dropping below the back fence and the chairs around the fire pit.

"I should clean up first."

"We can do that later. I want to enjoy the sunset."

~*~

They watched the sun drop below the distant mountains in silence. Hunter considered holding Mai's hand, but he had a rule about partners. Never get involved.

"That was great. I can't remember the last time I sat and watched the sunset." Mai sipped her wine as Hunter built a log fire for later.

"I'll be right back," said Hunter.

He returned with a bowl of ice cream, and a plate of Navajo fry bread with sugar, and a cup of coffee. Hunter loved sweets, and it seemed Mai did, too.

"All this beauty happens every day, and people are too busy to stop and enjoy life," said Mai.

"By people, you mean you and me."

"Who owns the lot behind you?"

"Sheriff Davenport, I think. I'm guessing he owns this whole block and several more. His family had a ranch here at one time. Why?"

"If someone built a house behind you, all this would be lost. Once it is gone, it never comes back." She turned away.

"Are you crying?"

"I'm sorry. This evening was so nice, and I don't want to ruin it. This case has me all tied up."

Hunter wasn't sure if the case was what made Mai cry. He didn't know what to say. He wanted to hold her, and he was certain she wanted to be held, but they were partners, and he had rules.

"Perhaps we should call it a night. We have to get up early."

"I think that is a good idea. I need to put my clothes in the dryer." She got up and walked back to the trailer without another word. Hunter cleaned up the grill and brought in the dishes and glasses. Mai called goodnight while he was washing up in the kitchen.

"See you in the morning," said Hunter.

In the movies, he would have followed her into the bedroom and made love to her. Or she would have stolen into his room later in the night saying she needed to be held. He knew neither was going to happen. *This isn't a movie,* he thought. It would never work, we are cops.

In his bedroom room, Hunter listened to the radio for a time. Eventually, he decided he wanted something sweet—candy or a cookie before going to bed. Slipping out of his room, he silently walked toward the kitchen. Sitting alone at the kitchen table with a glass of wine in front of her was Mai Yázhí. Not wanting to embarrass her, he crept back to his room.

Mai walked out of Hunter's trailer in Hanksville. Hunter was still asleep. She considered waking him, but she thought better of the idea. To the east, the sky had changed from dark black to a deep blue. Mai crossed the street and jogged north toward Utah Highway 24. It was five in the morning.

Mai set off at a moderate pace, warming her body against the morning chill. When she ran, she stopped worrying about her cases, her son, and her mother. She put one foot after another until she found her groove. During the day, she would not have run on a road with so little shoulder and so many blind turns. Now she had the road almost to herself. Finding her stride, she pictured Hunter Nalje. Not handsome. He reminded her of pictures of Geronimo—grim and determined, quick-witted, and decent. She had enjoyed their dinner. It had been so long since she had been out with a man alone. Last night felt like a date. She smiled. Then she remembered Alice Sweetwater. What must Alice be enduring? Mai had interviewed several of the victims of the Arches Rapist. The man's brutal cruelty and the humiliation they experienced were more than most women could live with. Mai had experienced beatings as a child; she could only imagine being sexually abused.

She stopped to survey her surroundings. What right did she have running for exercise while a madman held Alice Sweetwater captive? Mai turned back toward the trailer. She and Deputy Nalje had work to do.

~*~

Hunter was sitting at the kitchen table drinking coffee. He'd been waiting for Agent Yázhí for more than a half hour. A pot of coffee, a plate of scrambled eggs, and a basket of fry bread adorned the table. He wanted to call or knock on the door, but he was afraid she was hung over or worse.

At six, she came out dressed and ready to go. In fact, she looked very fresh and remarkably attractive in her washed and pressed clothes. "Sorry, my department head called," she explained. "He asked if we needed the FBI? I told him we could handle it. He reminded me; it's been four days."

"How long does she have?"

"Men who keep women captive follow a pattern. Many women stop fighting. They become numb to their fear. When that happens, the man gets tired of the woman."

"What does that mean?"

"They aren't fun anymore. I worked a case last year. A serial rapist. At first, he let the women go. He'd keep them for four or five days—perhaps a week—and then he let them go. He told each woman if she talked to the police he would find her and kill her."

"Didn't they see his face?"

"No. He had some kind of cabin. He wore a mask."

"At first, he raped and beat the women, but he let them go."

"And, later?"

"Strangled. I guess he got worried they would talk."

"Or, he needed the extra thrill."

"I'm worried about that. If Walt Fremont is just getting started, he might keep her alive longer. We shouldn't give up hope. We have to work harder."

"That's how I feel too. Do you want breakfast?"

"No, I ate cereal after my run. But I can wait if you want to eat something."

"It looks like we are both anxious."

~*~

They drove for an hour with little conversation. Yázhí talked to her department head on her cellphone, and she checked on the various stakeouts. Nothing. Eventually, Hunter had to ask about drinking wine at his kitchen table.

"I saw you last night," he said.

"I heard you. Why didn't you join me?"

"I'm not much of a drinker."

"And, you think I am?" She shifted in her seat to face him. "Or, did you imagine I wanted you?"

"I didn't think either. You are my partner, and I like you."

"At other times in my life, I might have been drowning my sorrow or waiting for you to make your move. I'm not a saint, but Alice Sweetwater comes first. The case has me all tied up. I could not sleep. I'm guessing, neither could you? You needed water. I had a glass of wine."

"Sorry. I should have sat with you."

"No, I'm glad you didn't. I might have done something foolish."

"Would it be foolish?"

"In the middle of a case? Yes."

"What about later? After we save Alice."

"How are you with kids?" Mai asked.

"I'm not sure, why?"

"No reason. How much farther to Lyman?"

"Not far at all, now."

"Should we call for backup?"

"A deputy is meeting us," said Hunter.

Two hundred and fifty people made Lyman their home. Over 95 percent were white. The town had half a dozen streets laid out in the typical north-south-east-west grid. Like all small towns in Utah, the LDS Church dominated the landscape.

Driving through town, Yázhí commented on the quality of the yards and homes. In most small towns in southern Utah, the homes were trailers, and the yards were filled with junk. These homes were one-story ranch houses with yards with grass and a few trees. Wallace Fremont's home was the exception.

Fremont lived in a ratty, white trailer near the east end of 400 South. On the east side of his trailer was a fenced-in horse corral. On the other side was a house built three-quarters below ground. Perhaps a leftover from the Cold War. A bomb shelter home built during the bomb tests at Los Alamos. After Walt's trailer, the next home was around the corner and half a block away.

They found Deputy Sheriff Blake Young waiting for them in his squad car. Blake usually worked the front desk and the jail. Chief Davenport sent Blake because technically, Hunter needed the search warrant in his hand, and Davenport didn't expect trouble. Deputy Young was the Chief's nephew. He was neat and careful if not the smartest officer. Most importantly, he didn't tell his aunt about her husband sleeping in the office, or his fishing trips. Blake Young liked being a small-town cop.

The trailer had a fence around it to cover a crawl space. After knocking several times and identifying himself and Blake as deputy sheriffs, Hunter used a credit card to force open the door. Blake Young followed Hunter inside. He had his service revolver drawn. Hunter wondered if Blake had ever fired his weapon outside of a shooting range.

The stifling air inside the closed trailer smelled of garbage and something stronger. Something dead. As a team, Blake and Hunter advanced through the trailer. They left Agent Yázhí guarding the front door. She had a Glock automatic at her side.

Fast food bags, empty cans of beer, milk cartons, and pizza boxes littered the dining room table in the kitchen. Food-encrusted plates filled the sink. An easy chair facing a new flat screen TV dominated the living room. A Comcast control box and a computer with cables were hooked to the TV. Dirty clothes and garbage covered the floor; a trail of litter and filth led to the bathroom and bedrooms.

"No one's been here in a while," said Young. The deputy left the trailer in a hurry. Yázhí followed him to stand in the door. Hunter guessed they both needed fresh air.

"We're missing something," said Hunter. He walked back into the bedroom. Like the living room, clothes and plates of food covered the bed. A new Samsung flat screen TV, at least 70 inches, sat on top of a dresser that looked like it came from the Goodwill. A dozen porn magazines littered the floor beside the bed.

In the bedroom closet, Hunter found T-shirts and jeans and a hunting rifle in an expensive hand-tooled leather case. Under the bed, he found a long wooden box with a lock.

"Agent," he called to Mai. "I have something."

"What is it?" she asked, as she walked down the short hallway. She had several tissues held to her nose.

"A box with a lock."

"Is it a gun case?"

"It might have been, but I found this." He pulled the rifle out of the closet.

"It looks too long."

"There is only one way to tell." Hunter opened a small buck knife and worked on the lock until it broke open. A gray foam meant to protect an object lined the inside of the empty box.

"The lance," said Yázhí.

"It might be. This is important."

"Hunter, you and Agent Yázhí should come outside." Deputy Blake stood in the doorway.

They exited the trailer.

"I think there is something underneath. That's the source of the odor." Blake pointed to the crawl space under the trailer.

"Do you have a light?" Hunter asked.

"Sure, why?"

"I don't want Agent Yázhí crawling under there without a light," said Hunter.

"Why would I crawl under there?" Yázhí asked.

"You're the only one small enough." He used the Diné word for 'small.'

She glared at him and then sighed. "Hold my vest," she said, taking off her vest. With the flashlight leading the way, she pushed her way under the trailer until only her boots stuck out.

"I have a body," she called out.

"Male or female?"

"It's a dog."

"What?"

"A dead dog. It is one of those little, yip-yip dogs."

"Rosemary Haller," said Blake. "Rosemary called in last week complaining that her dog, Billie, was stolen right out of her yard. I remember she talked to Chief Davenport. He talked to her daughter, too. Rosemary has a house at 100 South and 100 West. She lives alone. That is just around the corner."

"We may have solved the case," said Hunter. "Mai, you had better come out, we will let forensics take over. There may be more."

"Rosemary loved that little dog," said Blake.

"This is how a lot of serial killers start," said Yázhí, as she exited the crawl space.

"Blake, do you know Walt Fremont?"

"He's big and looks stupid, but he isn't. I hunted with him in high school once. He's patient. A watcher, and a crack shot."

"Anything else?"

"Town this small, everyone knows the gossip. Walt Fremont had a thing about Native Americans and little girls. Little blond girls."

"What about Native Americans?" Yázhí asked.

"Walt is all kinds of a bigot. White power and such, But not about Native People. He claimed he was part Apache. I heard that when his claim was denied, he was devastated. For a time, he worked at the Fremont Museum. Rumor had it he was a pot stealer."

"What about the blond girls?"

"Walt's wife, Gladys is LDS. She taught Sunday School until a parent complained about Walt helping Gladys with the girls in the bathroom. The bishop had a talk with him, and Walt stopped going to church."

"It fits with the porn in the trailer," said Hunter.

"We need to talk to his wife. Do you know where she is living?" Yázhí asked.

"Her folks moved to Torrey or Fremont. They are the Johnson's. Bob Johnson. I'll have to stay here and wait for the crime scene people, but you can check with the county clerk."

Hunter and Mai stopped at the County Court House and asked the records clerk, Cyrus McCandless, to check the land deeds for a

Robert Johnson. Even in a county with only several thousand people, the records listed seven men by the name of Robert Johnson. One owned two pieces of land, one in Loa, and one in Fremont.

"The Fremont Johnsons belonged to my ward. They are dead, a year now," said McCandless.

"What happened to their home, the one in Loa?" asked Hunter.

"Gladys is living there. I saw her buying groceries just the other day. I asked when we would see her at church again? She said something about how she was going back and forth between here and a place in Fremont," said McCandless.

"Is the Johnson place in Loa easy to find?" asked Yázhí.

"It's the last one-story house on 100 East.," said McCandless.

Hunter stopped by Sheriff Davenport's office to give him an update. The sheriff was lying on the daybed in his office reading the *Book of Mormon.*

"Would you like me to go with you to the Johnson house?" Sheriff Davenport asked.

"You are welcome to come along, but I'm sure we will be okay if you are busy," said Hunter.

"My grandson is playing baseball later this afternoon. I don't like missing his games."

~*~

The one-story wood frame house had a well-kept yard and a two-car garage, with a ten-year-old Honda Civic parked in the drive.

Agent Yázhí stayed at the truck, letting Hunter knock on the door. They didn't expect trouble, but there was no point in being careless.

It had taken five knocks before a boy with long hair and a beard came to the door.

"Yes," said the boy.

"Does Gladys Fremont live here?"

"Gladys lives in Torrey."

"Who are you?"

"Jerry Johnson. Who are you?"

"Deputy Sheriff Nalje. I'm looking for Walt and Gladys Fremont."

"What has Walt done now?"

"He's wanted for questioning. Where can I find him? Or, your sister?"

"Gladys and Walt have a trailer in Lyman. You should try there."

"We've been to the trailer in Lyman. When did you see your sister last?"

"Last Wednesday. Sometimes she visits on Wednesday or Fridays. She does her laundry, and visits Mom and Dad's graves."

"How about Walt? When was the last time you saw Walt?" Hunter asked, looking around the room. There were empty beer cans by the living room chairs and a knitting basket by a couch.

"At my parents' funeral. He got drunk."

"We understand your parents had a trailer in Fremont. Could your sister be living there?" asked Agent Yázhí. She followed Hunter's gaze to the knitting basket.

"She must be. She and Walt like to use both trailers. I'm not sure why."

"What's the address in Fremont?" asked Hunter, sounding anxious to leave.

"It is the second trailer on One Hundred West. It's a single trailer with a cement drive. If you get to Two Hundred South, you have gone too far."

Fremont was five miles north of Loa. Unlike her husband's trailer, Glady's trailer was neat and clean. Gladys turned out to be a large woman in her thirties. She wore a little makeup, but her hair had that beauty parlor look. The kitchen was spotless, and the living room had a radio and no TV. A pile of church books rested by an extra-large La-Z-Boy chair. After checking Yázhí and Nalje's identifications, she offered them lemonade and homemade cookies. The fresh scent of baking filled the room.

They sat at a kitchen table. She had a large glass of soda with 7-Eleven printed on the glass.

"Mrs. Fremont, we appreciate you seeing us," said Yázhí. "We understand you are separated from Mr. Fremont. Is that right?"

"For two years now."

"How long had you been married?" Yázhí asked. She took out a small, leather-bound notebook and wrote something on a new page.

"Four years. We met in high school. Wally was a different person then. He worked for the state, in a museum. He was a custodian. He's like you two."

"How do you mean?" Yázhí asked, her tone sharp.

"He claimed one of his great grandmothers was Apache Navajo. I never saw any proof. His mom was like me. She was from Mormon pioneer stock. His dad was white, too. He worked on the railroad. He traveled. Wally liked to say his family was named Fremont because they were related to some explorer. I guess that's how the town got its name, too. Another time he said his great-grandfather came here as a farmhand. He was Welsh and had some funny name, so he becomes Ian Fremont. The thing is Wally made up all kinds of stories. I could never tell the truth from a tall tale."

"Mrs. Fremont, I have to ask. We saw your husband's trailer, and it was different from your home." Mai Yázhí tone was softer, as if they were friends.

Hunter took the opportunity to stand in front of Gladys.

"Wally was always a slob, and it's Gladys."

"I beg your pardon?" Hunter glanced at Yázhí. She only smiled.

"My name is Gladys."

"Gladys, that's an unusual name. What's the origin?" Hunter asked.

"My grandfather was Welsh. You know, from Wales, in England. Just like Wally's. Gladys is from the Welsh name *Gwladus* or *Gwladys,* meaning 'royalty' or 'princess.' My father said I was his princess. It also means 'gladiolus flower.'"

"Wow, you know so much about your family," said Yázhí. She watched Gladys' eyes. She only looked at Hunter.

"It's because of the Church."

"You're a member of the LDS church?" Yázhí asked.

"I'm not active right now. It is because of Wally He liked to help me teach Sunday School. Folks in our ward didn't want Wally helping me with the kids. They said he needed to stick to the men's meetings. Wally didn't like that, so he left the church. Made me leave, too."

"Did he like young girls?" Yázhí asked.

"He likes blonds. He made me dye my hair. I had dark hair. Now I'm a blonde and I'm not having more fun."

"How did he feel about dogs?"

"He hates dogs, but he likes cats."

"We noticed your husband had several new flat screen TVs."

"He's addicted to porn. It's one of the reasons we separated. He'd watch porn and then want to…well, you know." She blushed and then became a bit dreamy.

"Did he make a lot of money as a custodian?"

"Wally received disability. But that barely kept us in food and rent. I can't imagine where he got the money for those new TVs. That one in the bedroom is as big as the bed."

Hunter started to ask a question, but Mai Yázhí cut him off.

"What museum did your husband work for?"

"At one time, he worked at the Natural History Museum in Salt Lake. Then at the Fremont State Park and Museum. That's where he was injured." She drank from the glass of soda.

"He loved talking about the ancient people. He even made arrow heads. He is very good with his hands." She giggled to herself.

"When did you see your husband last?"

"Three months ago, he came here. Said he was lonely. He wanted to be man and wife again. He'd been drinking, and I knew what that meant. It was sex he was after. I said I would take him back if he'd go to church and talk to my bishop. But he wasn't having it, so I had to kick him out."

Was that after you had sex, Hunter wondered.

"When was the last time you visited his trailer?" Mai Yázhí asked.

"Three weeks last Friday."

"But, you said—"

"Wally wasn't there. I still have the keys. We are still married technically." She sat straight up.

"I am not questioning your motives, I just need a clear timeline," said Yázhí.

"Wally owes me money. He wasn't answering my calls, so I went there. The place was a pigsty. You saw the place."

"Is there somewhere else your husband liked to go to get away? A place where he could be alone. A childhood place, or some quiet place?" Yázhí asked.

"We used to go camping near the Fremont Indian Museum in Richland. We would camp at this nice campground, it had toilets and showers. They even rent cabins. Ancient things fascinate Wally. He had a very large collection at one time. You might look there."

"Anyplace else? How about friends?"

"Wally didn't have many friends."

"How about other women?"

"Have you seen Wally? I mean, I still love him, but he has become something of a slob. He has really let himself go."

"So, no girlfriend?"

"Did I tell you he is obsessed with blond girls? In the grocery in Hanksville, there was this blond checkout girl. Wally talked about her all the time. I told you, he made me dye my hair. Like in Hitchcock's movie 'Vertigo'. He'd make me pretend I was a checkout girl. It was all disgusting. Sometimes I had to wear knee socks and pretend I was a school girl." For a moment, she seemed lost in thought. *She's remembering the sex*, thought Hunter.

"One thing about Wally. He called me his princess. I liked that."

"Is there anyone else we might talk to who would know where we can find Walt? A male friend?" asked Yázhí.

"Did you talk to Mel?"

"Mel, who?" Hunter asked.

"His half-brother, Mel."

"We don't have any record of a brother or half-brother."

73

"Wally's dad had several 'wives.' Mel is two years younger than Wally. Mel showed up one day saying he was Wally's half-brother. That was three years ago. Mel was twenty. Something like that. They used to go hunting together. Mel is a sweetheart. When he visited, he'd bring ice cream. You should talk to Mel. If it wasn't for Wally, I might be with Mel."

"Is his last name Fremont?"

"No, he said his last name was Burns, but he used other names like you Indians do. I just call him Mel."

"What do you mean, 'like Indians do?'" Yázhí asked.

"I meant no offense. But you people have your Christian names and your birth name and family name, and your adult names. It can be very confusing. Mel went by several names. Mel claimed part of him was Apache Navajo. Wally did too." She giggled again and put her hand over her mouth.

"Is there something funny?" asked Mai Yázhí. She was not smiling.

"I asked Mel one time what part of him was Indian, and he said the part he was saving for me." She giggled, again. "He can be very naughty."

"Where does Mel live?"

"The last I heard; he was living in Joseph by the park."

Yázhí stood up, and Hunter followed.

"You've been very helpful. I'm afraid we took too much of your time. If your husband contacts you, please call the local police, or call me or Deputy Hunter. And…"

74

"Be careful," said Hunter. "We are concerned that Walt has become violent."

"Wally wouldn't hurt me. That isn't his way. He could be rough, but sometimes rough is nice, too. Isn't it Agent?"

Yázhí ignored the suggestion. "Oh, one last question. Do you remember a neighbor, Mrs. Haller? She had a little dog?"

"That old lady was a bitch, she complained about our yard and the garbage. Wally would tell her to go to hell. One time Mel chased her with a buck knife. He said he was going to gut her like a deer. She picked up that little dog and ran to her house. She lives way around the corner. She complained all the time."

Hunter watched Gladys as she told the story about Rosemary Haller. She became a different person. Angry and unchristian.

"Why are you asking about Rosemary?"

"No reason. Thanks, again."

They shook hands and thanked her for the lemonade. Hunter took a cookie for the car. Just before he left, Gladys asked Hunter for his card, "In case I see Wally," she said, squeezing his arm.

Hunter had met women like Gladys before. Conservative, religious women who were convinced, "If he's red he's better in bed."

"Why didn't you tell her about the dog?" Hunter asked as Yázhí buckled her seat belt.

"I'm not sure. I think there is more she isn't telling."

"I know there is. The question is what?"

"She still loves him, or she wants him. I'm surprised she let you go. My guess is she is calling Wally or the brother right now. I wish we had a wiretap."

"Oh, I forgot something, I'll be right back." Hunter opened the car door.

"Should I turn the motor off?" Yázhí asked.

"Don't be silly."

He left the car, knocked on the door, and waited several minutes before Gladys asked him into the house. When he came back out, he was carrying his cellphone.

"You left your phone?"

"Wait." He touched a picture on the phone. The sound of some moving and then dialing a phone. Then Gladys said, "Mel, the police are looking for Wally. A couple of Indians. They are going to come looking for you. I told them you lived in Joseph and your name was Burns. That should slow them down at least for a time. I'm not sure what Wally has done, but they asked about that old lady, the one you chased." There was a pause.

"They are looking for the white camper," said Gladys. "Do you have it?" There was another pause.

"Tell Wally to watch out. You, too. And remember, I love you both. Bye."

It took the two officers several minutes to digest the recording. It couldn't be used in court, so the question was, do they go back in and grill Gladys, or find Mel, and leave Gladys under surveillance.

"Our girl Gladys has just become an accessory after the fact. What we need is a friendly judge. Is there a way to determine the number she called? You can almost hear the dial tones," said Mai.

"There is a guy in Loa who can get the number," said Hunter.

Hunter pulled out of the driveway and drove to the sheriff's office in Loa. Hunter took Mai in and reintroduced Deputy Blake and found her an office in which to work. She called the park service to set up a surveillance team. He left saying he had to see a guy.

Yázhí spent the next minutes arranging for a team of park service police to watch the house in Fremont. She also talked to Sheriff Davenport and asked him to send an unmarked car until her team arrived. By the time the surveillance teams were set up, it was after five in the evening. Mai knew the case could break at any minute. She understood that if she were in Moab, she would be too far away to coordinate the action. What if the mysterious half-brother Mel showed up, or Walt? Likewise, what if Gladys went to Walt or Mel? Nonetheless, she was anxious to get back to Moab, if only for a night. The deciding factor was Hunter.

Hunter had a friend who owned an electronics shop. When the sheriff wanted, a wiretap or to place a camera and bug, Clarence Jones was the man. Jones had degrees in electronics and criminal science. His shop was something of a curiosity.

Clarence listened to the recording twice before transferring it to his computer. He listened to it a third time while a computer app analyzed the tones. Clarence wrote down a number on a notepad. He handed the note to Hunter, saying "I think this is the number. Let's see what the computer says." He turned back to the computer waiting for it to come up with a number. When it finally did, he clapped his hands, like a little boy.

"I was right. That's the number. It's a cellphone. Do you want to check the owner?"

"I thought that was impossible," said Hunter.

Clarence gave Hunter a don't be stupid look. He spent several minutes on his computer before calling someone on the phone. Again, he took notes. When he finished on the phone, he handed Hunter his pad.

"The name on the phone is Malcolm W. Halah. I don't have an address yet, but I will have one in a couple of minutes."

Halah in the Diné language meant "brother" or "sibling." It was only a guess, but Hunter imagined the *W* was for Wallace or Walter. The half-brother's name was an Indian name meaning Wallace's brother. Likely it was an alias. He had Mel's phone. Now all he needed was an address. The phone rang. Clarence listened and wrote on his pad, and then thanked the caller and hung up.

"He lives in Green River. Here is the address."

He handed Hunter the pad. Hunter gave Clarence a hug and said he owed him. In the parking lot, he called Agent Yázhí.

"We are driving back to Moab," he said.

CHAPTER 8 - Saturday, June 11, 2016

Mai leaned down and touched her son's cheek. She hated to leave her infant, but the case needed her attention. The Green River Police verified that a man named Malcolm Halah lived at 415 North and 300 East. They offered to check on Halah, but Yázhí wanted to be present when a team entered the house. The plan was to send in a team of four officers at seven in the morning.

Mai picked up her Glock 19 off the bed and fitted it into her shoulder holster. She was wearing a bulletproof vest under a pullover top. To cover the gun, she put on a lightweight coat; the kind women wore over a dress. She had used the Glock in the service. For her, it was the perfect weapon. A good size and one with which she could hit a bullseye, seven out of ten times.

She grabbed a duffle bag on the floor and set it on the bed. She packed a change of clothes, a toiletries bag, and extra clips for the Glock. Whatever happened, this time she would be ready to stay in the field for several days.

She thought about Hunter staying at a nearby motel. On their way through Hanksville, Hunter stopped to change his clothes and pack a travel bag. He planned to stay overnight in Moab. Feeling rather awkward, Mai explained that she was staying at her sister's house, and there wasn't a room for Hunter. He said, "No Problem," and called ahead to get a motel room. When he dropped her off, she wanted to

79

invite him in, but she wasn't ready to explain about Ahote. Instead, she asked Hunter what time he would pick her up. Without hesitation, he said, "Five thirty."

~ * ~

Hunter stayed at the Super 8 where Alice Sweetwater had stayed. He worried they were losing sight of Alice in the search for Walt Fremont. This was her fifth day in captivity.

Hunter brought a bag of donuts and two coffees from Sweet Cravings in Moab. He wasn't sure if Mai Yázhí drank coffee. If she didn't, he would drink both. They had to be in Green River by six thirty.

Hunter had driven his Chevy truck rather than a squad car. The truck had four seats and he could play music on long trips. He had a good collection of rock and country music. He also had language tapes with singing and storytelling in the Diné language. One day, Hunter hoped he would teach his own son about Changing Woman and tell him the story in the language of the Diné.

Hunter picked up Agent Yázhí at her sister's house, on East Rose Tree Lane and Hillside. The small house had a carport rather than a garage. The house had two fruit trees and a white picket fence in front. Yázhí greeted Hunter from the door saying she would be right out. There was someone else with her. Her sister, he assumed. Yázhí left without closing the front door. She had her own bag of food and a travel mug.

"I brought coffee," said Hunter.

"Hot chocolate," Mai said, lifting her travel mug.

80

"How about a donut?"

"Yogurt and grapes."

"Very healthy. You didn't lock your door."

"I told you, it's my sister's house. She and my mother are taking care of the baby."

"What baby?"

"My son, Ahote."

"Ahote is a Hopi name. It means anxious, doesn't it?"

"Restless would be a better meaning. His father was very traditional. The women in his family named the baby when he was three weeks old. He was fussy that day."

"How old is he, now?"

"He'll be two in February."

"How come you never mentioned a son?"

"You never asked."

She removed the top of her mug. Steam escaped, and the car smelled of chocolate.

"What about his father?"

"Tommy died in Iraq. He never got to see Ahote."

"I'm so sorry."

"I should have told you all this before."

"It's okay."

She didn't speak for a time, and neither did Hunter. Finally, Mai talked about growing up and then about being in the military. She admitted to having been raised LDS but leaving the church when she joined the Army. Like Hunter, she served as an MP. However, she met her late husband Tommy in the park service. He was a park ranger and in the Army Reserves. She was twenty-six when they married and he was twenty-four years old.

Hunter wanted to ask why she married a Hopi, but he thought that was too personal. Hunter liked women, but he seldom dated, and he didn't think about marriage or a family. He believed in marrying for love, but he also respected the Diné rules about marrying outside of one's clans.

Yázhí belonged to different clans. With her sitting close to him, he realized once again she was very attractive. He wondered if a woman as attractive as Mai would consider going out with him. He wanted to ask.

A team of park service police was waiting down the street from the trailer when Hunter and Mai Yázhí arrived. Since Green River was in another county, a local deputy was at the scene. With men in the back and front, Agent Yázhí knocked on the door. She had her hands at her side. Behind her, Hunter held his gun against his leg.

"National Park Service," she called out. "Police, open up." When no one answered, she sent two officers to canvass the neighborhood. One of the neighbor told the officers Mel worked at the Gas-N-Go station. The neighbor said he hadn't seen Mel or the white camper in days. At the mention of the white camper, Mai Yázhí was on the phone having a warrant issued by a friendly judge

A call to the Gas-N-Go station owner confirmed that Mel had worked there, and that he hadn't shown up for work in three or four days. The owner also mentioned that for the last week, Mel's half-brother, Walt had been hanging out. Rather than wait for the warrant, Hunter and Yázhí drove to the Gas-N-Go.

"He is one of these big dumb-acting fellas, but creepy. He was always leering at the young girls. And, I mean young."

"Anything else?" asked Yázhí, making a note in her book.

"Some petty cash is missing. I assume Mel took it."

"What kind of cars are Mel and Walt driving?" asked Hunter.

"Walt has a 1997 Dodge truck with an add-on camper top. It's white. Mel has a 2008 Honda. Blue I think."

In less than an hour, they had a warrant issued by a local judge. Agent Yázhí and Hunter let the local police enter first to make sure no one was home. In the search, they turned up more porn, dirty dishes, and an antique firearm, a old Colt Peacemaker. Most interesting was a framed picture of Gladys, and a large packing box with native rugs, pots, arrowheads, and other artifacts. Mel also had a new flat screen TV, the same brand as Walt had in his trailer. The only thing missing was Mel.

They sat in the car. Agent Yázhí read her notes. Hunter listened to the radio; a local baseball game. "What now?" Hunter asked.

"The scent is cold."

"We should go back in the canyon."

"Rangers are there already. Two more eyes won't matter. Besides, I believe Walt and Mel took her out of the canyon. You are the hunter. Where is the best place to hunt?"

"Water helps. But the simplest answer is to wait where the prey gathers."

"What if Alice Sweetwater wasn't a chance victim?" Mai asked. "Mel works at a gas station in Green River. His brother was hanging around. His brother who likes blonds, and young girls. What if Alice stopped there for gas or a soda and Walt followed her?"

"She is young and blond. Gladys said he's attracted to blond girls," said Hunter.

"We have only her word for that. What else is Alice?"

"Mormon?"

"She is a Jack, but that could be important. What else?"

"Scientist. She's an archeologist," said Hunter.

"Right, she loves artifacts."

"And so does Walt."

"I think we should visit that museum Gladys mentioned."

"Why not just call?"

"I like to interview in person," said Mai. "Get a read on the person talking. I can't do that on a phone. I think it is important to talk to people who worked with Walt. Call it a feeling. I don't have a clear picture of Walt Fremont. Something is missing. Do you remember the museum's name?" Mai, took out her notebook.

"Fremont Indian State Park and Museum," said Hunter.

"Another Fremont? Where is it?"

Hunter spent a time studying a road map he pulled from the glove compartment. He pointed to a spot on the map.

"It's near Sevier, that's about two-and-a-half hours from here. If we hurry, we can get there before they close."

Mai took out her cellphone. "I'll call ahead and make an appointment with the director," she said.

The Fremont Indian State Park and Museum was twenty-one miles southwest of Richfield on Clear Creek road just north of I-70. They arrived after three in the afternoon. The red brick structure reminded Hunter of a school building. A half a dozen cars were parked at one end of the lot. At the reception desk, Agent Yázhí introduced herself and Hunter. She explained they had an appointment with the director.

The museum director looked more like a women's physical fitness instructor. She was small and lean with broad shoulders and muscled arms. She had very short, close-cut blond hair. She wore tights and a skirt. She had on what looked like rock climbing shoes.

"I'm Susan Vaughn," she said. "After you had called, your superintendent called my boss, and he called me. I am supposed to help in any way I can. Shall we go to my office?"

They walked past glass displays of primitive tools and weapons. The museum even had a native hogan cut in half. In Vaughn's office, animal heads, arrows, and spears decorated the walls.

"First," began Agent Yázhí, "do you know a student from USU named Alice Sweetwater? She is a grad student in archeology."

"Of course, Alice has visited many times. I'd guess she has been coming since she was a girl. Her whole life has been about studying ancient people and their artifacts."

"What about Wallace Fremont or Malcolm Halah?" asked Yázhí. She settled into her chair and pulled out her notebook.

85

"Mel's name isn't Halah. You two should have realized that was a nickname." The director laughed. "Mel is Wally's brother. Wally introduced him as Mel Kinnel once and Mel Bikinii another time. The joke was Mel had a house and Wally lived in a trailer. I'm not sure about Mel's real last name. I used to call him, Libahii."

"Gray one," said Mai.

"Mel has a certain level of raw charm. But he is a shadow of a man. He always looks so pale like he's a vampire. Wally is a different story. He seems simple, but he isn't. It is like he is acting."

"You seem to know both men well," said Yázhí.

"Wally worked for us for a while. He was a custodian. I'm guessing he would have worked for free. He was fascinated with arrowheads and spears. Just like Alice, he had been coming here for years. But something changed him."

"What happened?" asked Yázhí.

"Wally didn't show up for work for a whole week. The board wanted me to fire him. When he came back, he had changed. I was going to let him go, but then he had his accident."

"Why were you going to let him go?"

"Because of what happened with Betty Thomas, our receptionist."

"What happened?"

"She said Walt followed her in the bathroom."

"Was she raped?"

"No, Walt just followed her into the bathroom. He said it was all a mistake. There was no physical contact; no rape."

"Did you call the police?" asked Hunter.

"No, my board didn't want the bad press. I planned to talk to Wally, but then he had the accident. He fell while changing an overhead light and hurt his back."

"When was all this?" Hunter asked.

"In 2013."

"What can you tell us about Walt's half-brother, Mel?" Mai asked.

"It is hard to believe they are related," said Susan Vaughn. She seemed to smile at the thought. "Mel is very forward. The first day we met, he asked me if I would show him around. When Wally looked at you, he had this hungry look that made some women and girls uncomfortable. Mel was different; a little dangerous, but exciting, too."

Hunter and Mai exchanged looks.

"Did you go out with Mel?" Yázhí asked.

"We went hiking a couple of times. But when Wally left, Mel left too." She sounded sorry.

"What about recently, have you seen Mel or Wally?" Mai asked.

"No. What is this all about?"

"Alice Sweetwater is missing. Perhaps kidnapped. Two park rangers were shot," said Mai.

Hunter stood and walked to the window. Both women watched him. Outside the director's window was a large model of a Fremont village as imagined by scientists. Woman wearing simple white cloth dresses were grinding corn. Man in a loin cloth were making stone arrow and lance heads.

"Walt Fremont's white camper was seen at the scene of the crime," said Hunter. "He is what we call a person of interest."

"Naturally, I heard about the rangers. My heart goes out to their families." Susan Vaughn's tone was cool and matter of fact. She stood, so that she looked down at Agent Yázhí.

"I can't believe Mel or Wally could have anything to do with kidnapping or murder. That doesn't seem possible." The director looked toward her office door. She rubbed her hands on her skirt. "I'm sorry, but I need to leave. Is there anything else I can help you with?" She took a step toward the door.

"No. We've taken enough of your time. Is it all right if we talk to Betty, the receptionist before we go?" Yázhí asked.

"Betty...certainly. You can use my office. I'll send her in."

The director left, and moments later, Betty, the receptionist, joined them. She was a woman in her forties. Mai spent several minutes explaining why they were there. They talked about Wally and the bathroom episode.

"It might have been a mistake like Wally claimed. But the way he looked at me, that day, was really different. Creepy."

"Had he ever done anything like that before with you or any of the other women here?" Mai asked.

"No. I felt sorry for Wally. He seemed like such a lonely soul. It was his brother who I worried about."

"How so?" Mai asked.

"He was too slick for me, always flirting. Susan liked him. Liked him too much if you ask me." She looked around the room. "One time, I swear they had relations here in her office."

Mai gave Hunter a look. Fremont looked better and better. The question was how did Mel fit into the picture. She wrote "Mel?" in her leather book.

"Did you speak to anyone about Mel?" Hunter asked.

"I was going to talk to one of our board members. She is in my ward, but then the thing with Wally happened and then he was injured and gone. Mel, too. I didn't want to be a gossip. So, I said nothing."

"Have you seen Mel or Wally recently?" Hunter asked.

"The other day on Clear Creek Road, I thought I saw that white camper that Wally drove. I wondered if he was visiting Susan."

"Where was this?" Hunter asked.

"I was going west on Clear Creek. The camper was behind me. I saw it turn onto Trail Mountain Road. I remember because no one goes up that road except for hunters, but this isn't deer season. So, it was odd. The road goes to a reservoir. There is a place for hunters to park and camp."

"Is there anything else you can tell us?" Mai asked.

"I assume Susan told you about Wally's fight with the park service?"

"What happened," asked Hunter, looking again at Yázhí.

"I heard that a ranger caught a man collecting pot shards in Horseshoe Canyon. From the man's description, I assumed it was Wally."

"Was he actually arrested and sentenced?" asked Mai.

"No. The story is the ranger beat the hell out of him and told him if he found him pot hunting in the park again, he would turn him over to the tribal police."

"How long ago was this?" asked Mai.

"More than a year."

"How did you hear about the story?" asked Hunter.

"Alice Sweetwater told me. She has the hots for this young park ranger. He told her."

"Is there anything else you remember?" Mai closed her notebook. She was done.

"No, I should get back to work."

"Here is my card," said Yázhí. "If you see Wally or Mel or the white camper, call us immediately."

They walked to the reception desk together. Susan Vaughn was at the desk. Agent Yázhí thanked her for her time and gave her a card.

"Yes, but. . ." said Vaughn.

"Is there something else," asked Agent Yázhí.

"I don't have the deputy's card," said Vaughn.

"Certainly. My number is on the back." He handed her a card. Yázhí rolled her eyes.

They checked the museum parking lot and the two campgrounds associated with the museum. They didn't talk about the interview or the business card. Hunter watched the road, and Mai looked out her side window.

"You know who that old ranger was?" Hunter asked.

"I'm guessing, Cal Hitchens."

"No need to guess. He told me that story. He never mentioned the man's name. I should have realized. This whole thing could have been a setup. Alice was the bait."

"If she was just the bait, she's dead, and we are wasting our time."

"No, she is alive. The wall told you," said Hunter.

"You don't believe that."

"We have a lead, and the pieces are coming together."

"I'd like to see that reservoir."

"It's late. We should start back." said Hunter.

"We have another two or three hours of light."

"Should we call for backup?" asked Hunter.

"No, there is no reason to call in troops, yet."

"I'll call the office and let Davenport know where we are going," said Hunter.

The sign indicating the turn off for Trail Mountain simply read reservoir two miles. The road was narrow and steep at times climbing above the reservoir. On their way down, they saw a building with road equipment. Parked by the building was a Blue Honda. Hunter told Mai to call it in, while he used a pair of binoculars to scout out the area.

She spoke on her phone for several minutes.

"We aren't certain," she said. "There is no white camper. I know, but these guys killed two rangers. I'm not anxious for them to have a shot at another. We need backup."

"Well, tell your chief to send a local, but make sure they hold off on their sirens."

Off the phone, she frowned. "It will take more than an hour for anyone to get here. We need to act," said Mai.

"We need to be careful. We can't just drive in. There is no cover around the building. We wouldn't make it to within fifty yards."

"I'll drive in. Your car isn't marked. There is no sign you are a cop, and no one ever takes me to be a park ranger." She pulled off her vest and shoulder holster. From the back of the truck, she took out her bag and removed a pair of running pants and running shoes. Showing no modesty, she changed out of her uniform into a T-shirt, running pants, and shoes.

"I'll say I am lost. I'm looking for the road to Indian Peak."

"What will I be doing?" Hunter asked.

"Waiting for the reinforcements," said Yázhí. "Or we can go in together. We would just look like a couple of lost Indians."

"We should wait. This is bad policing," said Hunter.

"I can't. What kind of civilian clothes did you bring?"

"Same as you."

After arguing to no effect, he changed into shorts and a T-shirt.

"What about your shoes?" she asked, pointing at his Tony Lama boots.

"You won't laugh."

"Promise."

He put on his red moccasins.

"I'll drive," said Mai. "You can cover me when I go to the door. Take the map."

"What about your gun?"

"I'm counting on you."

They rolled the windows down and turned the radio up. Anyone in the building would hear them before they came into sight. Turning into the building's parking lot, Hunter got out the truck. He maded a big deal of looking at a map. Acting confused, he got back in the truck, and Yázhí drove right up behind the Honda. Hunter got out again with the map standing behind the open truck door. Yázhí got out of her door, again behind the driver's side door. On the driver's seat was her Glock 19.

"We are lost. We're on the wrong road," she screamed.

"We aren't lost. We haven't gone far enough," Hunter shouted back. He held the map in one hand, his automatic in the other.

"I'm going to ask," said Yázhí.

Agent Yázhí walked to the door and knocked. "Anyone there," she yelled.

"What do you want?" Someone called from behind the door.

"We're looking for the road to Indian Peak. Is this the right way?"

"You are on the wrong road. Go back to Clear Creek and ask at the service station by the museum."

"We have a map. Can you show us?"

"This is private property. You need to leave before there is trouble. My brother is coming back, and he hates Native Americans. You need to leave."

"Okay, we'll go. Look I hate to ask, but can I use your toilet?"

"No. If my brother found you in here, he'd shoot me. Use a bush."

Mai took a step back and looked around the parking area.

"Do you see any bushes? Can I go behind the house?"

"Do what you have to do, but be quick."

Yázhí went to her suitcase and pulled out a roll of toilet paper. She also picked up a small automatic that she carried in her purse. She hid the gun using the roll of toilet paper.

"I'll be right back. Why don't you drive the car around and pick me up, honey?"

She ran to the side of the building as Hunter closed the passenger door and walked behind the truck to the driver's side door. Again, he stood behind the door and waited a minute. Then he started the truck and drove around the side of the building.

Hunter was just in time to see Yázhí opening a backdoor. Not knowing what to do, he honked the horn twice before jumping out of the truck with a gun in hand. Yázhí disappeared into the building. Hunter sprinted to the door and followed her in.

Hunter was in a storage room. In the military police, Hunter learned to assess and control the situation. These were the primary rules for good policing. He took a moment to look around the room. A long work table with an industrial looking magnifying lens and two gooseneck lamps dominated the room. On the table were pots and pot fragments, arrowheads and stone knives mixed with and other native artifacts, packing crates, and bags of paper grass.

Agent Yázhí was standing in a shooter's stance in the doorway with the small automatic in her right hand. Yázhí yelled, "Police. Drop the gun. Drop the gun."

For a moment, Hunter thought it would be all right. Then he saw the barrel of an automatic placed against Mai's head.

"Deputy," someone called from the other room. "I am going to shoot your partner on the count of three if you don't drop your weapon and stand away. One, two. . ."

Hunter dropped his pistol. Agent Yázhí disappeared from the doorway. In her place was Mel Halah, still wearing his Gas-N-Go shirt and carrying a shotgun.

"It's all over Mel," Hunter said. "The police are on the way. There is no way out. Don't make this any worse. Drop your weapon, and I'll see you are treated fairly."

"That was an excellent speech, Deputy, but I have a gun, and you don't. With any luck, we will be gone before the cavalry arrives. Until then, I want you to raise your hands and come into this room. I have no reason at this moment to kill you or your partner, but I will if you resist."

Hunter raised his arms and walked into the front room. Agent Yázhí was sitting in a chair. A man in his twenties was tying her wrists with plastic zip ties. The man was tall and had on wire-rim glasses.

"Load the crates in their truck You can drive it. I'll drive the Honda," said Mel.

"What are you going to do with them?" asked the man.

"We are going to take the girl. We may need her. Put her in the back of the Honda. She can go with me. We are leaving in five minutes, so get moving. I'm going to talk with the deputy for a minute."

"What about Walt?"

"I'll call him. Get going and take her." Mel pulled Yázhí to her feet and pushed her to the man.

"There is no way out," said Hunter.

"Normally, Deputy, I would respect your professional opinion. But in this case, you really know so very little. I have hunted in these mountains for years. There are dozens of ways out of here if you know the area."

"What did you do with Alice Sweetwater?"

"Alice is with my brother. He is very fond of blondes. Me, I like darker women. Like your girlfriend. By the way, I didn't get her name."

"Her name is Officer, and if you harm her in any way, every police officer within a hundred miles will be told to shoot on sight. Give up now while you have a chance."

The tall man stepped in the doorway. "I'm ready," he said.

"Get in the truck and wait. I'll be right there." Mel waited for the other man to leave.

"Sit in the chair and put your hands behind you."

Mel used a pair of packing zip ties to restrain Hunter.

"You and I share a common ancestry," said Mel. "My grandmother was Navajo. We could be cousins, but here we are on opposite sides. In my heart, I want to let you live. But, then I remember what the guy on the TV news called you. Hunter, isn't that right?"

"Where is Alice Sweetwater?"

"She was right there. You were close enough to touch her," said Mel. He put the gun barrel against Hunter's head. Hunter closed his eye.

Mel tapped Hunter's head as if he was scolding him. "You had all the information you needed. But you got distracted by that bright little flower." Mel moved in close and whispered. "Have you fucked her yet? Your little flower. Or is that going to be my job?"

Hunter strained against the ties on his wrists. Mel hit Hunter on the side of his head using Hunter's pistol.

"You fucked up," said Mel. "We left Alice where you should have found her. That first day, you could have found her alive. Walt left her for you because she was nice to him as a kid. But now, who can say? She might be a ghost." He laughed and tapped Hunter on the forehead.

The truck horn honked.

"I have to go. My brother would have killed you, but, I'm going to let you live with the knowledge that Alice will die in the next twenty-four hours if she isn't found. The funny thing is, every minute you spend looking for Alice gives Wally and me more time with your little flower. You are sort of dammed if you do and damned if you don't. Now, I must leave, but a gift before I go. A remembrance."

Mel picked up an obsidian knife from a crate. He drew the blade down Hunter's cheek. Hunter cried out at the searing pain caused by the cut. He felt the blood flow down his cheek and onto his neck. He grit his teeth. He was determined not to cry out again. He focused on Mel, remembering every aspect of the man. For a moment, Hunter became Ma'iitsoh, the Gray Wolf. He had failed in protecting his partner. The role of the gray wolf in Navajo legend was protecting the tribe. Whatever happened, he would track down this man and kill him with his own hands.

CHAPTER 9 - Sunday, June 12, 2016

Mai struggled against the plastic zip ties binding her wrists. She was in the back seat in Hunter's truck. There were boxes of artifacts on either side of her. The tall man had gagged her and covered her with a Navajo rug. He talked rough and yelled at her, but Mai wasn't afraid of him. She was worried about Mel. She was certain he would have killed her if Hunter had not given up. *Hunter,* she thought. Was he alive? What would he do if he was? Would he go after Mai or keep searching for Alice Sweetwater? She hoped he would find the girl. That was his job. Her job was to survive and escape. To start, she had to pay attention to the trip. They were going uphill. She had hoped they would try to make it down to Clear Creek Road where the police would be waiting. Instead, they drove toward Indian Peak., the highest peak in the area. They must know a connecting road, or they had a place to hide. Mai forced her way into a sitting position. She tried to see out the side windows, but there was little to see.

They drove for several hours before stopping. Mel and a large man with long blond hair, who she assumed was Walt Fremont, carried her into a cabin. She saw a brilliant night sky, and other cabins on either side. They took her into a back bedroom and dumped her on the bed. The dark-haired man tied her arms and legs to the bedposts. Walt used a buck knife to cut away her clothing. For a time, both men stared in silence at her naked body. Walt had a hungry look Mai had seen interviewing convicted rapists. The other man, Mel, looked at her in a way that made her feel hopeless.

Nothing they do matters. I will survive, Mai thought. *I must.*

"You want her first?" asked Mel.

"You caught her," said Walt.

"Let's wait for Gladys. See what she wants to do."

"Gladys spoils everything for me," said Walt.

"Not for me," said Mel.

~*~

It took hours for the first officers on the scene to find Hunter. Sheriff Davenport issued an APB for Hunter's truck and dispatched a helicopter to search above the reservoir. On the drive to the courthouse, Hunter pictured the tall man with the wire-rim glasses.

Who was he? Hunter thought. *What was his relation to Wallace Fremont? What did Mel mean when he said, you had all the information you needed?* Hunter had no idea where to find Mai. *What if Alice Sweetwater was still alive? In the Canyon.*

Hunter arrived at the sheriff's office in Loa after midnight. So far, the investigation had focused on the white camper. Hunter and Mai had assumed Alice was in the camper. What if she never left the park? Mel said Hunter could have touched her. Hunter pictured the wall. He saw the dead dog in the grave. Why kill the dog? Why kill the dog and not the man—the owner of the station wagon. Two graves would have been just as easy as one. He wanted the man alive. He needed the man. Hunter sat back and reviewed what he knew about Fred Gerber, the owner of the station wagon. Nothing! He knew nothing. A good investigator turns over every stone. The search for the white camper and his interview with Gladys Fremont sent him to the museum. She sent him away from Fred Gerber, and away from Horseshoe Canyon.

Hunter checked his notes and found the address for Fred Gerber. He lived with his mother in a trailer at 350 North in Green River. It would be after midnight if Hunter went there now. Instead, he drove home to Hanksville. His cheek hurt, and so did his pride. He wanted to talk to Fred Gerber's mother. He wanted to know where Fred collected rocks.

Hunter arrived in Green River before dawn. At Gerber's address, Hunter found a clean, double-wide trailer with Gerber's station wagon parked in the drive. Hunter wondered who had towed the vehicle back and why it was here and not in the county impound lot. A week's worth of trash in barrels lay by the side of the trailer. A wooden crate with brown packing grass sat by one of the black trash barrels. Hunter walked up the three steps to the door and then thought better. He left his card in the door and then got back in his car and drove away.

Around the corner, he called the Green River Police and asked for a silent back up. In minutes, two officers arrived in separate cars. Hunter explained the situation and what he wanted. Hunter borrowed a vest from a police car. The officers guarded either side of the trailer while Hunter knocked on the front door. When no one answered, Hunter called for a warrant.

With the warrant in hand, Hunter stepped up to the door and again knocked. He had his foot ready to kick in the door, when a woman's voice called out, "Yes?"

Hunter lowered his pistol to his side.

"Police, we are looking for Fred Gerber."

"Fred's not here. He's at the store."

"Who are you?"

"His mother."

"Mrs. Gerber, please open the door."

A woman in her sixties opened the door a crack. "Fred's at the store."

"Can I come in?" Hunter pushed the door open at the same time showing her his badge and the warrant.

"I have nothing to hide. I've just been watching the BYU channel on the TV."

"Where is the store you mentioned?" Hunter asked. He looked at a row of pictures displaying a tall boy wearing wire-rim glasses. In one, the boy was holding a large piece of quartz.

"Fred has a rock and antique store north of town just before the highway entrance."

"Does your son know a man named Walt or Wallace, or a man named Mel?"

"Walt and Fred go rock hunting in the canyons. Mel is Walt's brother."

"We found your son's car in Horseshoe Canyon. He was reported missing. How did the car get here?"

"A man in a tow truck dropped it off. I don't understand. Fred isn't missing."

"What is your son driving now?"

"He has my Volkswagen. Is something wrong?"

"What did your son say happened in the canyon, and where is his dog?"

"Dog?"

"You told the police he was walking with a dog named Ginner."

"Yes, I don't really know what to say. Fred got her from the pound only the day before he went camping. I never thought he liked dogs. He told me the dog ran away."

"Mrs. Gerber. Does Fred have a gun?"

"Fred, a gun. Yes, he has a hunting rifle."

"Can I see Fred's room?"

"I don't understand what you want?"

"Just a look." Hunter walked to the bedrooms without waiting for an answer. There was a large flat screen TV in both bedrooms and on the wall in the second bedroom hung a replica of a prehistoric lance. At least, Hunter hoped it was a modern fake.

~*~

The rock shop was a single room building made of corrugated steel. A sign in front read Rocks, Fossils, and Antiques. The shop was closed and locked. There was a glass display case outside, and a long wooden table with large stones marked for sale. Hunter and a local deputy sheriff search the area for any sign of foot traffic or vehicles. They found tire tracks close to the front door.

"We need to know if he comes back here or shows up at home."

"I'll keep men on both, but I think he has flown. What are you going to do now?" asked the deputy.

"I'm going with a team back into the canyon."

"How many days is it?"

"It's going on seven."

"No one can live that long out in that maze without water."

"I'm hoping she has food and water."

"Why would someone do that?"

"So, he can have sex with her when he wants."

~*~

The searchers met at the trailhead sign. Ten sheriff's officers, and another ten rangers from the park service.

"I want to thank you all for getting here on such short notice," said Hunter. "I am Deputy Sheriff Nalje. I have reason to believe that Alice Sweetwater is still alive and being held in a cave or hidey-hole by Wallace Fremont. Fremont is armed and dangerous. It is likely Alice has very little time left."

"What about Agent Yazhi?" asked one of the park service officers.

"Who are you?"

"Officer Custer Tsinnie, National Park Service. I am Bit'ahnii, born for Táchii'nii. My cheii is Honágháahnii and my nálí is Dzil tahini."

"Agent Yazhi is being held by Fremont's half-brother Mel and another accomplice we now believe to be the missing hiker, Fred Gerber. Gerber has a rock shop in Green River. His mother informed me that her son went rock hunting with Walt Fremont. His photo matches one of the men who took Agent Yazhi."

"Why do you think Alice Sweetwater is here?" asked Tsinnie.

"Mel said she was still in the canyon. He said I could have touched her the day I searched. My guess is she is near the Ghost Gallery in a camouflaged hole or cave. My plan is to search in pairs. We'll start at the Great Gallery and fan out from there."

It took less than thirty minutes to walk down the trail and reach the canyon floor. After that, they moved in pairs, always with one armed man watching for an ambush. They were looking for any sign of digging, and any hidey-hole in the rock wall. They established a control point with water and an ATV. From there, they searched the side of the canyon where they found the dog. This time they focused on the rock walls, looking for any possible crack or cave. They moved on both sides of the canyon with half the men walking along the river bed and another half walking along the cliff face.

Hunter followed Tsinnie and another officer as they moved along the long wall of painted figures. There were over twenty big figures and many small paintings of animals and men in several hunting scenes. Along the Great Gallery wall was a ledge with small caves and large cracks. No one had any idea how to reach the caves without ropes or ladders. A ranger assured Hunter that an ordinary ladder wouldn't reach, and the ledge to the larger caves was less than a foot wide.

"Can we get a ladder that will reach?" Hunter asked.

"The fire station might have one. I'm not sure," said Tsinnie.

"What about those caves?" Hunter asked, pointing to the largest above the paintings.

"We know people lived in them at one time and used them for ceremonies, but no one's been in them for years, perhaps centuries."

"Is there a way to get to that ledge?"

"A good climber might make it to the ledge or repel down from the top, but that doesn't seem likely. If there is a hidey-hole, it is below the figures or half way up. The thing is. . ."

"What?"

"It has to be a natural hiding place because no one found it in all these years."

A police whistle sounded south of the wall. Hunter and Tsinnie ran to three men standing by a group of massive boulders just beyond the wall with the paintings.

"What is it?" asked Hunter.

"We have a small hole," said a ranger.

"And?"

"It has a painted canvas flap."

"How did you find it?" asked Hunter.

"The color on the flap has faded. It's a different color from the rock."

"How do we get in?" asked Tsinnie.

"Not through the flap."

"Did you call in?" asked Tsinnie.

"First thing, I did. No answer."

"Let's circle these boulders. The entrance must be near," said Hunter.

It took half an hour before someone got on top and found an entry covered with more canvas and gravel. Once cleared, the opening resembled the entrance to a hogan. They didn't have a ladder, so they lowered one of the officer with a flashlight into the hole.

The ranger dropped to the cave floor. The darken cave was big enough for two adults. There were pot fragments under the ranger's feet. Reaching using his light he found Alice leaning against one of the walls.

"She's here," he called. "I'm afraid we are too late. We will need a crime scene team down here."

"I want to see," declared Hunter.

They had chained Alice to an iron loop screwed into the wall. She was naked and bruised. An empty water jug lay next to her body. Someone had stacked her clothes in a pile. Hunter knelt beside her bound and gagged body.

"I'm sorry," Hunter whispered. "You didn't deserve this." He brushed a blond curl away from her face. Her cheek was warm.

"She is still warm. Are you sure she's dead?"

"I didn't feel a pulse," said the ranger.

Hunter poured water from his drinking tube onto his fingers and wet her lips. "Do you have a mirror, let's check for breath."

"I don't have a mirror."

"Call for the doctor."

Minutes later, one of the team's medics dropped down into the space. He and Hunter helped the other man back out using a makeshift rope ladder.

The medic spent several minutes listening and testing the body.

"She's alive, but I'm not sure we can get her out alive. She is so weak. It is possible I can start her on an IV in here, but we'll need a medivac."

"I'll call it in. You start the IV."

Hunter took off his jacket and covered her body.

An hour passed before they carried her to a waiting helicopter.

When Alice was gone, Hunter called the searchers together.

"First, I want to thank everyone for what you did today. The three men we are after are monsters. What they did to that woman is unspeakable. Now, we must find Special Agent Yázhí. She has been a captive for a little over a day. There is still time." Hunter's voice quivered with emotion. He took a moment to gain his composure.

"It is possible they will turn up at one of their homes, and we are watching for them. It's also possible they have other hidey-holes like this cave and that is where they have Agent Yázhí. The third possibility is they will bring her here. We must be ready for that possibility. That means we must leave this place as we found it and post enough watchers to catch them if they return."

"Can't we post a guard at the trail head?" asked one of the officers.

"We'll need a guard at the gate, but these men are pot hunters. My guess is they can come in by several other ways. Maybe they'll use an ATV and drive up the river bed from the south."

"That's illegal," someone called out.

Everyone laughed.

"This is murder and big-stakes pot sealing. My guess is they aren't worried about breaking the park rules."

"They could use horses. There are horse tracks all around," said Tsinnie.

"Odds are they come in at night. They could dig for an hour or so at first light, and still leave before any hikers arrive."

"We should have someone in the cave, and three men outside."

"You will need someone at the trailhead and another at Hans Flat."

"That makes five men. We can rotate who is at the trailhead, but we will still need five to seven men to mount an adequate guard."

"Two teams, including those at the trailhead."

"We'll need supplies," said Tsinnie.

"I'll take care of the supplies," said one of the park rangers. "Who's going to stay down here?"

"I will," said Hunter. Six other men raised their hands. Three rangers, a deputy, and two tribal police officers.

~*~

National Park Service Ranger Andy French volunteered to wait in the hidey-hole. He had agreed to stay there all night. Deputy Tom Andersen was a hundred feet to the south. Like Hunter, he made a makeshift blind. Andersen was from Emery County. The other three men were sleeping in a sheltered area they found about a half a mile east. They would relieve the men at the boulders at three in the morning.

Hunter pulled a horse blanket around his shoulders. It was one thirty at night. The high desert was cold after sunset, even in the hottest part of the summer. Hunter's father liked to say the sand and limestone gave their warmth to the moon. The earth's heat lights the moon, he claimed. Hunter had his Winchester on one arm, and his pistol in its holster. He longed for a cup of coffee and a cheese sandwich, but nothing was going to distract him from his vigil. He sat with his back against the cliff wall some hundred feet north of the boulders. Earlier, he'd cut cottonwood branches and made a simple blind, the kind that he might use when hunting deer or ducks.

When Hunter was a boy of twelve, his father and grandfather took him on his first deer hunt. On that trip, Hunter's father insisted that they hunt with a lance, and bow and arrow. Hunter thought the idea foolish when they could use a rifle. He wasn't very good with a bow, but he could throw a lance and his grandfather taught him how to use a sling to send a lance twice as far and twice as fast as he could throw.

"When you kill a living thing," his father explained, "it is very important that you understand the nature of your act. With a rifle, you

110

can kill a deer from a mile away. The deer never sees or hears you. He has no chance. With a lance or the bow, you must be close. So, close, the deer can smell you. To kill a deer, using a bow and arrow you must move with the wind. You must use your senses and your brain. Killing a deer with your bow or the lance will prove you are ready to join the circle of men. You are ready to be a man."

"But one arrow isn't enough to kill a deer," Hunter said.

"That is why you have a knife. You must chase down the deer and finish him with your knife. The arrow is enough to kill the deer eventually, but he will die in pain. In fear. Your knife gives him release. Today, you will use a special ceremonial knife. My grandfather gave me a stone knife. The handle was from the horn of a deer killed by my grandfather's grandfather. The obsidian blade is older than that. Made before the time of Changing Woman."

That day Nalje shot his first deer using a bow and arrow, and then he chased the buck until he and the deer could run no more. Hunter knelt beside the buck and asked the spirits to accept the deer into the world beyond. His cut with the stone knife was clean. The deer bled out, and Hunter's father declared his boy a man, he called his son Hastiin Nalzheehii, Man Hunter.

Tonight, Hunter was again hunting, this time he was hunting men. There was nothing noble in his task. He would use his rifle to kill without giving them any warning. Hunter sat with his eyes closed. He listened to the night. In the distance an owl called out, then all was silent with just the wind through the cottonwoods. Hunter wondered if they were wasting time. With so many places to watch, had he chosen wisely?

The sound of a motor, like a motorcycle or ATV, broke the silence. A pair of lights were moving up the river bed from the south. Hunter could make out a rider, but he wasn't sure if he was alone. The plan was that the other officers would take their cue from Hunter. He would signal for them to close in. Whatever happened, no one was leaving the boulder.

The ATV pulled up close to the secondary entrance to the cave. The rider got off. He stretched, and then he pulled something out of the back of the ATV. It was a telescoping ladder. He put it against the boulders. From the ATV, he took out a rifle and a water jug. He used the rifle sling to put the rifle behind his back. In the moonlight, Hunter saw the glint of the man's wire-rim glasses. Fred Gerber.

Hunter wasn't expecting Fred. He assumed it would be Walt who came for the girl. The rock collector started up the ladder. He had a flashlight in his right hand and the water jug in the left. The climb was awkward. Hunter called out the cry of the coyote. Gerber stopped and then continued up. Hunter stood and stepped out of his blind. He had the rifle pointed at Gerber. The guard from the south was standing behind the ATV.

Gerber pulled the cover off the hidey-hole. He pointed the flashlight down into the hole. Immediately he dropped the water jug and tried to bring the rifle around. Hunter pointed a powerful flashlight at Gerber. The other two rangers did the same.

"Fred Gerber. This is Deputy Sheriff Hunter Nalje. You are under arrest. Put your hands up and stay where you are. There are four rifles pointed at you. Any false move and we have orders to shoot."

Gerber turned off his flashlight and put his hands in the air. Andy French stuck his head up from the hole.

"Throw your rifle down," he shouted.

French had a pistol in his right hand. Gerber made to set his rifle down as French pushed his way out of the hole. Gerber stood and kicked French in the face. Officer French dropped out of sight, and Gerber slid down the back side of the boulders.

Hunter moved to his right toward Gerber. A shot rang out. Hunter was surprised one of the others had fired. A second shot rang out. It seemed too far away. Hunter looked for the guard who had been by the ATV. The ranger's flashlight was on the ground. Hunter pointed his flashlight at the boulders, nothing. He pointed his light back to the ATV; the ranger was on the ground by the vehicle.

Hunter turned his flashlight off and let his eyes and his ears adapt. His senses would find Gerber. To his east, two flashlights' beams were moving, running, toward Hunter. Another shot rang out and one of the flashlights appeared to tumble.

"Turn your lights off," Hunter yelled. "Gerber is loose and armed." Without thinking, Hunter stepped to his right and dropped to the ground. A shot rang out as a chip of rock broke on the wall where he had been standing.

Hunter put his rifle behind his back. He pulled out a skinning knife from a sheath on his belt. He crawled forward ten feet before he was up and running to the ATV. Close to the vehicle, he made out the man on the ground—one of the guards. Another figure was climbing onto the driver's seat.

The man was searching for the keys. He had a hand on the throttle. Hunter grabbed the man from behind and dragged him back off the seat. Fred Gerber. Hunter placed the knife blade against Gerber's throat and drew blood. Hunter wanted to kill the pot stealer but finding Yázhí depended on taking Gerber alive.

"Lie still or I'll cut your throat."

Gerber struggled. "Fuck you," he called out.

He tried to raise his right hand. He had something in his hand keys, a knife, perhaps a gun. Hunter slashed the knife across the man's hand. Gerber cried out, even as he struggled to get free.

Hunter punched Gerber in the face. "Lie still," he screamed.

A flashlight beam illuminated Hunter and Gerber. Tom Andersen stepped into view. "Deputy, are you alright?"

"Put out the light," Hunter shouted.

Andersen gave him an odd look. A stain of red spread across his uniform blouse. Andersen crumpled to the ground.

"For a man named Hunter, you aren't very smart," said Gerber. "Let me go, and you might survive, this. Walt and Mel are hunters, too."

Hunter drove his skinning knife into the center of the man's thigh. "You aren't going anywhere." He flipped his automatic around and struck Gerber hard on the back of his head. He was immediately silent and motionless. Hunter pulled a pair of plastic zip tie cuffs and attached Gerber's hands behind his back. Hunter guessed the rock collector had twenty minutes before the knife wound would be a serious concern.

Hunter crawled away from the ATV. Somewhere out in the darkness was Walt, and possibly Mel. Also, there was a park ranger a tribal police officer, plus Andy French, the ranger in the cave. They needed to gather and plan. Hunter gave his coyote yelp. This was answered by an owl hoot. Hunter knew the owl was Custer Tsinnie.

Hunter looked at his watch. It was four fifteen. They had another hour before first light. Hunter crawled to the cliff face. The Ghost Wall was visible in the moonlight, the legless spirits floating above the canyon floor. Hunter touched the wall, willing it to speak to him. Hunter blinked. For a moment, it seemed one of the painted figures moved; then it moved again. It was Ranger Tsinnie with a blanket around his shoulders. He was sliding along the wall. Hunter admired the stealth and cleverness of the older man. During their time searching for Alice, Hunter had discovered they not only shared membership in two clans, but Tsinnie also believed their paternal grandfathers were likely blood relations. Learning of their possible family relation, Tsinnie started calling Hunter, Nephew. Out of respect for the older Navajo man, whose family name meant bony one, Hunter started calling Tsinnie, Uncle.

A shot rang out, and Tsinnie dropped out of sight. *That shot was close*, thought Hunter. He looked back at the ATV. There was a man dressed in black sitting on the seat of the ATV. Gerber was on the ground. The ATV sputtered to life. The man leaned down half off the seat. It looked like he was offering his arm to Gerber; like he was offering to help Gerber onto the ATV. Instead, a gun flash exploded next to the rock collector's head. The man gunned the ATV and drove off even as Hunter fired four bullets at his back.

Hunter listened to the motor fade in the distance; aware that there could be another shooter somewhere in the dark. Hunter returned to wall. The dead, like the ghosts, were going nowhere.

When the first beams of light touched the canyon rim, Ranger Tsinnie crawled to Hunter's spot at the wall.

"It is good to see you alive, Uncle."

"And you, Nephew. The ghosts watch over us."

"Do you think they are still out there?"

"There is only one way to tell." The older ranger stood.

"Rangers. Deputies. Call out your status," he yelled.

"I have a broken leg," called Andy French from the boulder cave.

"Deputy Johnson. I'm safe, but I ain't moving."

"What about the boy who was with you?" Hunter shouted.

"He's dead. So is Andersen."

"I'll call for help," yelled Hunter.

He called for help on his radio. He could have called earlier, but he wanted to be sure the first responders would be safe.

"This is Deputy Sheriff Nalje in Horseshoe Canyon. We need immediate medical assistance for a man with a broken leg. We have four men down."

"Say again," said the dispatcher.

"Four dead, three officers and one of the suspects."

"Can you move the man with the broken leg? Over."

"I believe so. Over."

"Okay, a helicopter will be there in thirty minutes."

"How's the girl?" Hunter asked.

"She didn't make it."

 Mai awoke with a start. Gladys Fremont was sitting on the bed. She was washing Mai's body with a hand towel. Gladys had a bar of soap and a glass of water. She was humming a Disney tune while she worked. Mai struggled to free herself from the zip ties around her wrists.

"It is no good struggling, Agent Yázhí. Mel is very good at tying women to beds. He tied me a few times." She giggled. "I shouldn't say this, but Mel and I are talking about going to Vegas. I love Walt, and I honor our wedding vows, but there is just something about Mel. He takes a girl's breath away. Walt is nice, too, but everything must be just right for him. Otherwise, he gets angry. That's why I'm washing you." Gladys set the towel down.

"Walt likes a clean woman, and he needs you to fight. He can't get it up anymore unless you beg and fight. If you fight, it will be over in no time. If you don't, he might just quit and leave or he might beat or kill you. I shouldn't be giving you advice but fight at first and then when he is aroused enough to enter you, play dead. Go all limp, and he will too. But whatever you do, don't look at him or let him kiss you. That is my job." She set the glass and washcloth down.

"Walt, honey, she's ready," Gladys called.

~*~

Sheriff Davenport closed his office door. Hunter sat opposite the sheriff nursing the bandage on his cheek.

"Hunter, I am taking you off the case. This business in the canyon will be a problem." The sheriff wasn't angry. He his voice broke with emotion. "I had to tell Andersen's wife and his mother. I don't want to have to tell your mother, too."

"These men are killers," said Hunter. "They have Agent Yázhí because of me. It is my fault. There must be something more I can do?"

Sheriff Davenport put his arm around Hunter's shoulders. "Son, the park service, the FBI, the State Police, and the Tribal Police are all involved. They have a team of rangers hunting in the park, and men searching the hills above the museum. They don't need a small-town cop to help. I want you to take two days off. Get away from this mess."

"What about Agent Yázhí?"

Davenport sighed. "She's dead, or as good as dead. You saw the Sweetwater girl. This is Yázhí's fourth day. Her time is running out. I'm sorry Hunter, but I'm taking you off the case." The sheriff stood away from his desk. Hunter realized Davenport didn't care about Mai Yázhí. He had written her off.

"This is Monday. I want you back in the office on Friday. I'm not going to ask for your gun or badge or any of that Hollywood stuff. You are a deputy sheriff and I expect you to act like one. Now go home."

119

Hunter got in his squad car and drove to Hanksville. He wanted to be a good officer and follow orders, but Davenport was wrong. He had to do something.

~*~

Hunter's neighbor, Kim Wheatley, was standing outside Hunter's trailer. There was an old Chevy truck parked in front. Custer Tsinnie was leaning against the truck talking to Wheatley.

"Kim," said Hunter, greeting his neighbor with a nod.

"Hunter. I've been jawing with your, uncle. He says you had a tough couple of days."

"Yá'át'ééh, Uncle. To what do I owe this visit?"

"Man Hunter, it's good to see you. What is the news?"

"Likely you know more than me—I'm off the case. Sheriff Davenport wants me to stay home."

"I'll leave you two to talk," said Wheatley, making a quick exit.

"It seems we are both off the case. Perhaps it is best. The State Police and the Feds have their own way of doing things. We are just two Indians." He laughed.

"What is the word on Officer French?" asked Hunter.

"He may walk with a limp. But he is alive," said Tsinnie.

"No thanks to me. I should have realized an ambush was a possibility."

"I've been thinking about what happened. Those boys are smarter than I gave them credit, but I'm not sure it was planned as an ambush. I think the second man was left as a rear guard. He sent

Gerber in with water for the girl. When we sprung the trap on Gerber, he came in and fired at the flashlights."

"That makes as much sense as anything," said Hunter.

"Nephew, a man can only fight what he sees. You found the girl. Your family named you well. You shouldn't give up."

"What can I do?"

"The question is what can *we* do."

"You and me?"

"I've been thinking about that ATV. What's the range of an ATV?"

"In two-wheel drive on flat terrain, it probably would get one hundred miles to a gallon of gas."

"What about in four-wheel drive?"

"I'd expect twenty miles or less to a gallon."

"Did you see any spare gas cans?"

"No. I see where you are going," said Hunter. "But if Walt Fremont owned an ATV, it should have been at his trailer or at Gladys's house."

"That's one possibility. What if he stored it with a friend or someplace close to where he enters the canyon? What is the nearest town?"

"Caineville is west of the park trailhead," said Hunter. "But there is no direct road. Hanksville is the closest, in fact, if you are going to the park by way of Hans Flat, you could use a back road that begins two blocks from here. It goes out of Hanksville to Hans Flat. The thing is, Hanksville isn't very big. I'd know it if Fremont owned an ATV that he stored in Hanksville. I know everyone here who hunts or owns a gun."

"Still, it is worth asking around. Who should we ask?"

"You were talking to him. My neighbor Kim knows everything and everyone in this town. At least if it is illegal or there is money involved."

"Can we talk to your neighbor?"

"Come inside. I'll make you coffee and go get Kim."

~*~

"My rough count is ten ATVs here in Hanksville, but no one is storing an ATV around here," said Kim Wheatley. "There is a farmer who has a fairly new Honda ATV in Caineville. Also, there are two outfitters who rent ATVs in Fremont and Lyman. Even more in Loa and Torrey. I would talk to Fremont's neighbors."

"I agree," said Tsinnie. "I think we should drive over to Lyman where Walt has that trailer and talk to some locals. Find out the gossip about Walt and Mel. Do you like to fish?" asked Tsinnie.

"I do," said Hunter.

"I hear there is good fishing on the Sweetwater and all along the Fremont River. In Lyman for example. The problem is, I don't really know Lyman. Do you?"

"Not really," said Hunter.

"Let me make a few calls, get the names of a few locals, who speak the language," said Tsinnie.

"What should I do?" asked Hunter.

"Pack a bag. We could be on the road for several days. Oh, and Nephew, we might want to go hunting, too. We might need a friend, or two."

"I have everything we will need, but can we take your truck, all I have is a squad car, and I am supposed to be off duty. What year is that truck?"

"It is a 1970 Chevy. It is a C-10 with four-wheel drive. A classic."

"How many miles?"

"Two hundred and fifteen or so. But only fifty thousand from the last engine rebuild."

"I'm surprised it made it to Hanksville," said Hunter.

"I drove it to Salt Lake last month."

"Good enough for me, Uncle."

"I am honored, Nephew."

"Would you like a coffee for the drive?" asked Hunter.

"A chocolate malt sounds better. I don't suppose there is a Milt's in Hanksville?"

"Something almost as good, and I'm buying, Abízhí."

~*~

Once the idea of being nephew and uncle was established, the two men fell into a comfortable pattern of being related, even though their mothers were from different clans. Driving, they talked about their lives growing up, and about being a cop. When Hunter brought up what Mai must be experiencing, Tsinnie kept saying, she was "tough—a professional."

Passing a mile marker, Hunter asked, "How long have you been a park ranger?"

"I went to college for a year, but I wasn't a good student. Then, I joined the Navy and transferred into the Marines. Eventually, I became an MP."

"I did, too—Army."

"What a Navajo from Utah is doing guarding a destroyer in the Persian Gulf, I can't tell you, but I liked the service. I liked police work. When I got out, I kicked around for a time. A friend from my clan worked as a tour guide at the Grand Canyon. He got me a job. Because of my service and my skill with firearms, I was sent for more law enforcement training. Sometimes I fill in at the information desk or give tours to little kids, but most of the time I'm working on a drug case or cases involving weapons in the parks. This will be my thirteenth year."

"I hope you aren't superstitious."

"No more than most."

"Have you worked with Agent Yázhí?"

"We've met. I worked with her husband some. I liked him."

"I like her," said Hunter.

"I don't blame you."

"It's my fault. I surrendered my weapon."

"Nephew, we live with our decisions and our mistakes. One time I was called into a ranger station to break up a domestic fight, some argument between this Anglo and his wife. They were in the parking lot. He was drunk, and he had hit her a number of times.

Several visitors called it in. When I got there, he was passed out, and she was sitting in the driver's seat crying. I took her information and asked her if she wanted me to arrest her husband. She said no, he was a decent man when he wasn't drinking. She would get him home. I remember thinking she was making a mistake, but I am not married, and not likely to be, and I don't drink. So, I sent her on her way."

"Did he kill her?"

"No, he hit a family of eight while he was driving drunk. His wife was killed along with the other family. He was found on the side of the road passed out."

"It wasn't your fault."

"We live with our decisions but, we are defined by the choices we make."

They stopped at the Bureau of Land Management Henry Mountain Field Station in Lyman before going to Fremont's trailer. Tsinnie introduced Hunter to Jacob Chandler. Jacob was part Navajo on his mother's side. Like Tsinnie and Yázhí, he was Honágháahnii (One-Walks-Around Clan). After exchanging greetings and explaining their purpose, they asked Jacob about Wallace Fremont and his half-brother, Mel.

"Wally is a pig. We were in school together in Loa, his wife, Gladys, too. For a time, they were in my ward. Wally always claimed he had Navajo Apache ancestors, but he didn't, really. He was pure white trash, and she was even whiter. Gladys was a decent girl until she met Wally. Her parents were very upstanding in the church. She is one of these girls with a taste for the bad men."

"That fits," said Hunter. "Does Wally have an ATV or a friend with one?"

"A lot of folk around here own ATVs."

"How about a relatively new Honda ATV?"

"You might want to drive around Wally's trailer and Gladys' house. See if a neighbor has an ATV or a trailer in their drive or in the yard. If Wally has an ATV, it could be stored with a neighbor. Another thought is the Capitol Reef Outfitters in Loa, Bicknell, and Teasdale are possible, too. The outfitters rent ATVs. And, don't forget the towing companies. The three towing companies have one locked impound yard they share. That impound yard is one of the places where local folk store their campers and RVs. The yard is at Hunt's in Hanksville. It's right across from the ward house and the pioneer church."

"Anyplace else?"

"That's all I got."

They drove to Walt's trailer. There was crime scene tape across the door, and that was all. No police, no surveillance. There were three ATV owners in the blocks near the trailer.

Hunter and Tsinnie spent the morning talking to neighbors and asking the same questions. They worked their way back toward Hanksville. At each little town, they checked with any outfitter, towing company, and gas stations. In Loa, Tsinnie did all the asking. Hunter stayed in the truck. In Teasdale, they talked to a man with a new Honda. He mentioned his dealer said someone bought a new Honda for his ranch. He thought the rancher was in Fruita or Craineville.

"You might ask at the gas station down the street," the man said, pointing to the Phillips 66 next to the Broken Spur Motel. "That's the first gas station between Hanksville and here. If you had a ranch in Fruita or Craineville, you'd come here for gas."

They talked to the manager at the Phillips 66 on the outskirts of Torrey. He mentioned a farmer named Frank Langwell. "Old Frank's been coming here for a long time," he said. "Before me. Lately, he's been filling his truck and then two of those five-gallon containers. A couple of times, some kid came in driving Frank's truck did the same."

"Does Frank have an ATV?"

"Like I said, Frank has an old pickup and this new four-wheeler. Every so often, he comes in for groceries, driving the ATV."

"Is it a Honda?"

"I think so."

"Where does Frank live?"

"Near Grover. He raises cattle."

~*~

The sign to the farm read Langwell Farm and Ranch. They stopped on the road and used Hunter's binoculars. The Langwell farm was typical of a small ranch in southern Utah. An old wood-framed house, a garage/work shop made from corrugated steel, and a once red-painted barn that now was the color of gray, weathered wood. Outside the house a Ford pickup from the 1970s had weeds growing out of the tires. There was nothing moving, just some chickens in the yard.

"We have to check the barn."

"They could be hiding there. It's a perfect spot."

"I'll drive in. They don't know me," said Tsinnie. "You can come in on foot or stay low in the back seat."

"Let's try the back seat."

Tsinnie drove in with Hunter under a blanket in the bed of the truck. Tsinnie stopped in front of the house, walked to a screen door, and knocked. A curtain in a front window moved.

"What do you want?" someone called.

"I'm looking to rent a four-wheeler to do a day of bird hunting. The boy at the Phillips station said you had a Honda ATV," said Tsinnie.

"He's mistaken."

"You don't own an ATV?"

"I didn't say that, Chief. I ain't renting my Honda. I need it here."

"It's just for the day. I'd pay good money."

"What's wrong with your truck."

"Not legal where I want to go."

"How much will you pay?"

"Two hundred for one day. But I have to see the vehicle first."

"Okay, I'll come out."

Tsinnie stepped back to the truck and waited by the passenger door. An old man in coveralls stepped out of the house, leaving the door open. The man looked to be in his seventies. He had on cowboy boots and a straw cowboy hat. "It's in the workshop," he pointed to the garage. "Not sure why you can't use that Chevy."

"Can I see the Honda?"

They walked to the workshop. The old man pressed a button and a double garage door opened. Inside was a collection of work benches and woodworking tools and a relatively new Honda ATV.

"Have you used it recently?"

"What does that matter?"

"It looks new, but it's covered in mud and red clay like it has been used pretty hard and recently."

"I drove it to town yesterday."

"Do you live alone?"

"What kind of question is that?"

"The ranch seems like it might be too much for one man. I was just curious."

"You ask a lot of questions. Now let me ask you one."

"Go ahead."

"Are you the police? You can't lie."

"I am a park ranger with the National Park Service if that matters."

"I want you out of here, right now. I don't cotton with no police, especially, Indians."

"Is there anyone else in the house with you?"

"My nephew is visiting."

"Can I talk with him?"

"You can leave now."

"What's your nephew's name?" asked Tsinnie.

"Why are you here?" the old man asked.

"A Honda ATV was used in a crime. I am just doing a routine check. The man at the Phillips gas station said you have an ATV and here it is, and it looks like it has been out in the canyons. If you like, I can get a search warrant and be back in twenty minutes. If your ATV has been used in a crime, we will take it and anything else we find that might relate to the crime. Guns, for example."

"I don't think you heard me. I want you off my property." Langwell walked over to a gray cabinet, opened the double door, and pulled out a Winchester Pump Action. "I ain't asking, I'm telling."

Tsinnie started toward the truck with his back to Langwell. A boy in his twenties stepped onto the porch. He was barefoot and had long hair and a very long uncombed beard. He had a hunting rifle in his right hand.

"Is there a problem Uncle Frank?"

"No problem," called Tsinnie.

"He's a cop," yelled the old man.

The boy pointed the rifle at Tsinnie.

Hunter pushed off the blanket and sat up, pointing his pistol at the boy. Tsinnie dropped to the ground.

"Son," Hunter shouted. "I am Deputy Sheriff Nalje. I want you to lower the rifle." The boy pivoted and pointed the rifle at Hunter.

"Drop the gun, Ralph," Langwell shouted.

The boy pointed the rifle at the ground. Tsinnie and Langwell walked to the house. Hunter climbed out of the truck bed with his pistol at his side.

"Is there anyone else in the house?" asked Tsinnie.

"Just me," said the boy.

"Mister Langwell, we need to check the house."

"What if I say no?"

"Like I explained, I'll get a warrant and then anything we find—illegal drugs or guns. Anything will be—"

"You have my permission. Just take it easy with the boy."

"No problem. Tsinnie, you wait here with Mister Langwell. Ralph and I will check out the house."

"Wait. Mister Langwell, do you know Wallace Fremont or his half-brother Malcolm?" asked Tsinnie.

"Walt Fremont. What does he have to do with this?"

"Do you know them?"

"Ralph knows Walt. His wife, Gladys, she taught his Sunday School."

"What about the ATV?"

"Ralph's been using it. He has been running the farm for me."

"Is he growing marijuana on the farm?" Hunter asked.

"Well."

"It doesn't matter. We are not interested in drugs. We are looking for Walt Fremont. Ralph, have you seen Walt or his half-brother Malcolm?"

"I've loaned Mel the ATV several times when he wanted to go hunting. He pays me."

"Pot hunting?"

"I don't ask."

"When did you see him last?"

"Yesterday about noon. He used the Honda overnight."

"Where did you meet?"

"At the gate to the farm."

"Was he alone?"

"No, he had a woman with him. She was waiting in his car."

"A Navajo woman?"

"No, it was Gladys Fremont. He paid me two hundred, and they left."

"What was he driving?"

"He had this pretty new Chevy truck with a white camper top, I think."

"Did you see in the camper?"

"No."

"Which way did they go? In what direction?"

"They went west."

"Good, now let's look in the house." Hunter handed Tsinnie his pistol. Tsinnie had a knife in his left hand held at his side.

"Mister Langwell. Walt Fremont and his half-brother, Mel are wanted for multiple murders. They are very dangerous. You and your nephew need to be careful. The ranch would make a perfect spot for them to hide."

Hunter reached back in the truck bed and pulled out his own Winchester and a second pistol, a Glock automatic. He nodded to Tsinnie before going into the house with Ralph. The inside of the farmhouse smelled of marijuana. Hunter noted the living room had another new Samsung flat screen TV. The house had a large kitchen, a separate dining room, and two back bedrooms. Keeping a gun on Ralph, they inspected each room in the house, before returning to the front living room.

"Ralph, I should warn you. If you have been doing anything with Walt Fremont or Mel—any kind of business—you need to be careful. These men are wanted for murder. If you've intentionally helped them, that makes you an accessory to murder and kidnapping. In less than an hour from now, a whole shitload of police are going to descend on you. If I were you, I'd get rid of anything that might put you or your uncle in jail." Hunter pointed to a bong sitting by the TV.

"Thanks."

"One more thing. Where did you get the TV?"

"Best Buy in Salt Lake."

"Are you sure? I noticed Walt and Gladys had new TVs just like that."

"So?"

"If I find out you've been pot hunting or selling artifacts, I will turn you over to the Tribal Police."

"I'm not afraid of jail. I've done time."

"I'm not talking as a deputy sheriff. I'm talking as a member of the Honaágháahnii, the One-Walks-Around Clan. The tribal police and the Feds take a very dim view of pot stealing."

"Okay, I sold some pots to this guy in Green River."

"Fred Gerber?"

"I don't know his name."

"Tall man in his twenties, with wire-rim glasses."

"Right. Look. I couldn't resist. He offered five hundred dollars and a TV. I won't do it again. I'll tell him I'm finished. No more pots."

"I am not worried about Gerber."

"Why not?"

"Your pal Mel put a bullet in his head because he wasn't useful any longer. He'll do the same to you or your uncle when he finds out you have helped the police. If you know more than you're telling, you better talk now. Do you know where Walt is or where Mel was going? Do they have a place they like to hunt or fish? Maybe a cabin?"

"Mel talked about going to Vegas for a weekend. He said he and Gladys were going to live it up."

"Thanks, you have an hour, use it well."

Walt Fremont and Mel Halah sat outside of their cabin enjoying the summer night. Mel lit a second doobie while Walt poured more rye whiskey into their glasses. In the high desert, the nights could be cold. Walt had on a pair of jeans, a flannel shirt and camo hunting vest.

Mel had on the same clothes he wore in the canyon: black jeans, and a black T-shirt. Splatters of blood dotted his jeans. He had a one-hundred-fifty-year-old chief's blanket around his shoulders. In Santa Fe or Scottsdale, a blanket like this one would bring ten or twelve thousand dollars. Walt took the blanket off a display at the museum and replaced it with a less valuable rug from the storeroom. No one seemed to notice.

"You better wash those jeans," said Walt.

"Gladys will take care of it," said Mel.

"When are we going to Vegas?"

"Friday, maybe sooner. It depends on selling a few pieces."

"Without Fred?"

"He was a weak link. It's you and me, Bro," said Mel. He handed Walt his joint.

"We will need new IDs and credit cards," said Walt.

"There is a guy. I'll call him tomorrow."

"What about Gladys?" asked Walt.

"I'll take care of Gladys. You take care of the girl."

"Do you want another shot at her?" asked Walt.

"She doesn't fight enough. You need to get rid of her."

"I'll take her into the Canyons."

"Beautiful night. Gonna be a full moon. I think the Diné call this a Buck Moon because bucks start to grow their antlers now. Maybe I'll give it to the girl one more time. In honor of the moon," said Mel.

"Beautiful night for it," agreed Walt.

~*~

Ranger Tsinnie called the Park Service Headquarter in Moab on Tuesday morning and spoke to the new agent in charge. Special Agent Sam O'Dell. Tsinnie made up a plausible story close to the truth without mentioning being with Deputy Nalje. He didn't bother to mention the nephew or the marijuana they found at the Langwell ranch. The investigators would discover both. He said he thought he had found the ATV that had been used in the Horseshoe Canyon shoot-out. He also informed Agent O'Dell that Gladys Fremont had been seen with Mel Halah, and she should be considered an accomplice. Finally, he mentioned Hunter's white twin cab Chevy truck, now with a white camper top. Tsinnie insisted that an APB be issued saying the fugitives might be driving to Vegas. When asked, he said he'd be back in Moab in a day or so, a small lie.

"What do you think about Mel being with Gladys?" Hunter asked.

"Where there's smoke there is fire."

"Do you think she and Mel are on their way to Vegas?" asked Tsinnie.

"It's possible. What bothers me is we haven't seen Walt. Mel and Fred Gerber in the canyon, and Mel and Gladys going to Vegas. Where is Walt?"

"He's guarding Yázhí. But that isn't the question."

"What is?"

"Why is Gladys involved?"

"She has a thing for bad boys. She's doing a Bonnie and Clyde." Hunter laughed.

"I don't believe Walt or Mel could have seen her in Loa without the police catching them. She knew where to find them."

"That means she shook a police tail."

"And, now she's an accessory to murder. Is she that stupid?" asked Tsinnie.

"I think she was acting the whole time we talked to her."

"Is it money or sex?"

"Probably both."

"So, what now?"

"We should go back to Loa and check out her trailer."

"Tomorrow is Wednesday. I wonder if she is still doing laundry at her parents' house?" asked Hunter.

"Now that is a good idea," said Tsinnie.

They drove to Loa but found no sign of Gladys at the trailer. A police car arrived while they were looking in the windows.

"What are you boys doing?" an officer called from his car. He stood behind his car door. Hunter put his hands in the air. He let Ranger Tsinnie identify himself.

"Gladys Fremont was seen with her brother-in-law. We're just checking to see if she is really gone."

"I thought you were off the case, Hunter," said the officer.

"Ranger Tsinnie asked me to show him around. We should have called ahead."

"Were you two involved in that fight in Horseshoe Canyon?"

"Yes."

"It sounds like these boys are on a killing spree. The word is, they have a park ranger with them. How's a thing like that happen?" the officer asked.

"Bad luck, I guess," said Ranger Tsinnie.

"Bad police work if you ask me."

"Have you seen Gladys Fremont?" Hunter asked.

"She'd be under arrest if I'd seen her."

"Just be careful. She's an accessory to murder. She has little to lose."

Hunter and Tsinnie spent the night at the Broken Spur in Torrey. They could have gone back to Hanksville, but Tsinnie had a friend who got them the special "Federal Rate" for a room. He and Tsinnie ate steaks and fry bread and bowls of ice cream. For a time, they sat outside at the pool and talked about the case. Always on their thoughts was Mai Yázhí. They planned to go early to the Johnson house. They had no plan beyond that.

Hunter came out from the motel room in the morning. It was after six. Tsinnie handed Hunter a police vest. Tsinnie had a vest on under his tan uniform shirt.

"Think we'll need these?"

"Better safe. . ."

"When we go back to Moab, I'd like to check in with Mai's sister. Mai has a son. I want to be sure he is okay."

"You're a good man, Nephew."

"I can't forget what that city cop said about bad policing."

"This is a new day. Let's see what Coyote has in store for us."

Torrey, Utah at seven in the morning was quiet. They drove by the Johnson home and continued to the next street. The Honda Civic had moved. It was on the other side of the drive.

"That's funny," said Hunter.

"What?"

"The Honda was on the right-side last time I was here."

"So?"

"I park my truck on the same side every night. The only time I don't is when I have visitors."

"Or if someone is parked in the garage and wants to be sure of a fast getaway. Should we call for help?"

"It's pretty slim. Besides, if we go all SWAT on them, more officers will be shot, and they'll kill Mai."

"Should we check in with the locals, or just wait?"

"We need a backup in case someone leaves, and we need to follow."

"Park around the corner, and I'll make a call."

Tsinnie said nothing more only they should wait. An hour later, two older Native Americans drove by in a beat-up Nissan sedan. They parked down the street and out of view from the Johnson house. Two minutes later, two boys on bikes rode by and stopped by the Nissan. Tsinnie drove the truck down the street and parked next to the boys.

The two boys had on blue pants and white cotton shirts. They had on name badges, and one had a *Book of Mormon*. One of the men got out of the Nissan.

"What's this," asked Hunter.

"Let me introduce Cadet Haskin and Cadet Clah," said the man. "I'm Sergeant Sam Lapahie, and the handsome officer in the front seat is Ben Nabahe. I assume you are Tsinnie, and you are the one they call Hunter. We understand you need a little unofficial assistance."

Hunter leaned into the truck to shake Officer Nabahe's hand.

"Officer," said Hunter.

"Yá'át'ééh I am Ben Nabahe. My mother was Kinya'áii (Towering House People). My father, Dzilt'aadí. My grandfathers were Tązhii dine'é and Bit'ahnii."

Sam Lapahie had not been exaggerating Officer Nabahe was handsome. He was also at least fifty and lean with those hard-chiseled cheeks that one associates with women playing Indians in the movies.

"We are related. I am Bit'ahnii, too," said Hunter.

"I called Sam," said Tsinnie. "He is with the tribal police. But he is stationed in Page and works out of Bryce. Before that, he was like me, an MP in the Marines. When I explained our problem, he said he had a solution."

Sergeant Sam Lapahie was older than Tsinnie. He was a large Navajo man with a barrel chest. His black hair worn in a Marine buzz cut was showing signs of gray. His police uniform seemed a size too small. Taller and bigger than the other men, he immediately took charge.

"You want to see who is inside that house," he said in a whisper. "No one is going to question a pair of missionaries handing out the *Book of Mormon*. Haskin has been on a mission. He knows what to do. Clah is going to play the silent Indian."

"Are they wearing vests?" Hunter asked.

"No, we tried them on under the white shirts, but they stuck out," said Sam.

"Are they armed?" asked Tsinnie.

"They are just going to do a look see. They aren't going in the house. They know the risks. These are my best students. They will be alright," said Ben.

"Where will you be?" Hunter asked.

"I'm going to be parked at the other end of the street," said Sam. "You go back to your watch post. The boys will have a look see, leave, and go to the next house, and then they will go around the corner. When they do, we can meet there and decide what to do next."

When the two cars were in place. The cadets rode their bikes to the house at the end of the street, one house away from the Johnson's house and walked up to the door and rang the bell. Hunter watched as they talked with an old man in his bathrobe. Soon they walked back to the bikes and over to the Johnson house. Again, they

141

stepped up to the door and rang the bell. At first, there was no response. Then someone came to the door. Cadet Haskin talked for several minutes, and then Cadet Clah handed someone a *Book of Mormon*. The two walked back to their bikes and repeated their call on the next house down the street before riding around the corner and out of sight.

The boys were talking excitedly with their sergeant when Hunter and Tsinnie arrived.

"There is a small, dark-haired man and a woman with short red hair. The woman asked questions that showed she was LDS. She questioned why the bishop would send us? She's smart," said Haskins.

"Is she going to run?"

"I don't think so," said Cadet Clah. "I said we were checking on her brother. It had been a year since he'd been in church. I asked if she planned to join the ward. She said she was just there for the day. The man said nothing. He was like a hawk. Watching."

"Did you see the boy, the brother?"

"Someone was watching TV."

"You did fine work. You will be a credit to the tribal police," said Tsinnie.

"Thank you, Uncle," said Cadet Clah.

The boys nodded to their sergeant and rode off toward the center of town.

"Do we wait, or call in the troops?"

"Let's see if they run or stay. If they run, we can follow, and if need be, I'll call in a road block."

"Why not call in the Feds and let the SWAT team go in?"

"We aren't sure about Walt. Is he there too with Agent Yázhí? Or is he waiting somewhere else with her? I'm worried about the brother. Is he an accessory or an accomplice?"

"How will you decide?"

"How long does it take to do laundry?"

~*~

They didn't have to wait long before the garage door opened and Hunter's Chevy truck, now with the white camper top, pulled out. In the truck was Gladys Fremont sporting short red hair. Mel was at the wheel and wearing a white cowboy hat.

Tsinnie called Sam and Ben. Tsinnie and Hunter would follow Gladys and Mel. Lapahie and Nabahe would arrange for a tribal tactical team to enter the house. The hope was that Gladys' brother was unharmed and willing to provide information.

Gladys and Mel left Torrey driving west toward Lyman and Loa. Hunter wondered if they were going to Gladys' trailer, but they continue west into Sevier County. The traffic on Highway 24 allowed the followers to stay back a quarter of a mile and still maintain a good visual on the truck. The only danger was they would pull off suddenly or stop and Hunter and Tsinnie would have to pass them and wait. An hour north of Loa, they turned west on Highway 119 toward Elsinore.

"They are going back to the museum," said Hunter.

"My guess is they have a hiding place in one of the towns near the museum. Where did Walt live when he worked at the museum?"

"I don't know, but I can find out."

"Let's check with Sam and Ben before you do."

Sam Lapahie picked up on the third ring. "Lapahie," he said.

"Sam, it's Tsinnie."

"The house was clear. The boy left in the Honda five minutes after his sister. We picked him up two blocks away. He acted like he didn't know what we were talking about. I informed him about being an accessory after the fact, and he caved. He said his sister and Mel were there for a night eating and drinking and having sex. He said Gladys said she was leaving Walt for his brother."

"What about Agent Yázhí or Walt?" asked Tsinnie.

"Claims he knows nothing."

"Where was he going?"

"For groceries. We searched the house. Nothing obvious, but we are going to hold the boy for a day, see if he remembers more."

"Sam, does Sheriff Davenport know?" Hunter asked.

"We had to let him know what we were doing. The park service too."

"Did he say anything about me?"

"He said you were off fishing. He didn't sound very convincing. He said he hoped you'd catch a big one."

"I do too."

"We could pick these two up. Make Mel talk," said Tsinnie when Hunter was off the phone.

"I hope they are taking us to Walt."

The couple drove past Elsinore and Joseph without stopping. When they reached I-70 they turned west again. Hunter was convinced they would stop at the museum or take one of the back-county, dirt roads. Instead, they continued to I-15 taking it south.

"Shit," said Hunter. "What county is this?"

"Beaver, I think. At least that is the next town of any size."

"We need to call ahead and organize a road block. I think they are going to Vegas. For all we know, Walt is dead. This has gone too far."

It took time for the sheriff in Beaver to understand what was happening and organize a plan. He sent a car to the Super 8 near the Texaco station in Beaver. Most people heading south got off at that exit for gas or food. If they did get off, the sheriff's car would block them on the exit, and Hunter and Tsinnie could come in from behind. Otherwise, the sheriff was arranging for a road block sixteen miles outside of town at the Fremont road exit. There were no exits in between, and the additional miles would give his deputies time to set up.

As luck or fate would have it, the fugitives took the exit to the Texaco station before the patrol car was ready. It was just coming around the Super 8 when Mel and Gladys drove by on their way to the Texaco and pulled in at one of the gas pumps on the side for cars. On the other side of the station were a dozen big rigs headed for Vegas or Los Angeles.

The Chevy pulled into the gas station. Hunter and Tsinnie had stopped the local patrol car before it entered the station. The deputy's name was Douglas Richland. He was on the phone to his sheriff when they drove up.

"The sheriff wants to let them gas up and leave. We can follow them to the road block."

"What if they don't get back on the Highway? What if they have lunch or take a surface road?"

"How dangerous are they?"

"He's very dangerous. We're not sure about her," said Tsinnie.

"There are too many civilians in there. Too many trucks and truck drivers. It could be a blood bath. We should just wait," said the Deputy.

"What if we go in on the truck side?" asked Hunter. "We need gas. We won't take any action. Just watch. You can stay here. When they go south, you can follow, and we will catch up before the roadblock. Give me your cellphone number. If they do anything unexpected, I'll call."

Hunter didn't give the deputy time to debate. He and Tsinnie drove off for the Texaco. The truck side of the station had a dozen trucks at the pumps or parked on the side. The station included a restaurant and convenience store. Hunter stopped at one of the outer gas pumps.

Tsinnie got out and used a credit card to purchase gas. Hunter could see the front of Mel's truck at a pump on the other side of the station. The Chevy was still there when Tsinnie finished filling his truck.

"They must be in the store or the restaurant."

"They could be using the restrooms."

"Should we check?" asked Hunter.

"Not unless you put on a vest, and I call it in. The deputy was right. Too many civilians," said Tsinnie.

"Maybe we could ask a truck driver to check for us."

"Too risky, Nephew. Mel doesn't know me. I'm going over to the rig with the *W* on the side. I'll make like I am asking the driver something. From there I can see inside the truck. If they leave, you can drive to me."

Tsinnie went to the truck and pulled out a Utah Jazz ball cap that he put on his head. He also put a pistol behind his back while Hunter used the time to put on a bullet-proof vest under a light jacket.

When Hunter was ready, Tsinnie strolled across the gas pumps to a rig with a Big W on the side. Tsinnie was talking with the driver when Gladys exited the convenience store on the truck side. She was eating an ice cream. Using her free hand, she shaded her eyes from the sun. She was almost directly across from Hunter who was sitting in Tsinnie's truck. Gladys took another bite of ice cream and then seemed to look around. She started toward the pumps and then stopped and went back in the store. Moments later Mel and Gladys came out of the door on the other side. Gladys was still eating her ice cream. Mel had a map in one hand, and a can of soda in the other. The white cowboy hat shaded his face. Mel stopped to push the hat up off his nose. He was in line with Tsinnie and the *W* rig. Tsinnie turned away as if to talk to the driver.

Mel dropped the map and soda and grabbed Gladys. He pulled her in between himself and Tsinnie and drew Alice Sweetwater's Glock Automatic from his waistband. Mel had fired at Tsinnie before his arm was pointed straight. A headlight on the rig exploded. Mel fired again, and Tsinnie seemed to fly backward into the side of the driver's door. This put Tsinnie out of a direct line of fire. In that moment, Mel let go of Gladys and started toward Tsinnie.

Gladys screamed, "Mel baby, come back. We have to go." Mel advanced on the ranger with his right arm straight out and supported by his left. Mel was in between the station and the pumps. He should have fired, but he didn't. He moved forward for a better shot. He couldn't see Hunter behind him, but Gladys did.

"Behind you Mel," she yelled.

Mel was turning back to face Hunter when Tsinnie shot him in the right shoulder, sending the Glock to the ground in front of Gladys. Mel had a surprised look and then seemed to plead with Gladys using his eyes.

Gladys picked up the Glock and pointed it toward Mel and then Hunter. She made a grunting sound, with the effort to pull the trigger. The bullet hit Hunter in the chest and drove him off his feet.

The shot that killed Gladys came from Deputy Richland. He was out of his patrol car in a shooter's crouch. It was the first time he had ever used his weapon against another person. He looked as if he might retch, instead he called in, telling the dispatcher he had shots fired, and two officers down.

Hunter staggered to his feet, advanced on Mel, kicked the Glock away from Gladys, and ordered Mel down to the ground. His chest hurt, but the vest had saved him. Hunter did a careful search of Mel, finding a second pistol and a buck knife. Using Deputy Richland's plastic zip cuffs, Hunter tied Mel's hands behind his back, before going to Tsinnie.

The ranger was sitting against the driver's side front tire. He held a towel from the truck driver on the top of his shoulder. It was soaked in blood.

"He got me just above the collar bone."

"So much for vests."

"When I tell this story to new rangers, I'll say the vest saved my life."

"It certainly saved mine," said Hunter.

"I can't imagine why she picked up the gun."

"True love."

Mai Yázhí woke from a dream. She had been washing her hair in a waterfall in a canyon. The dark room smelled of spoiled food, urine and feces, and semen. It had that acid quality of sweat and fear. Mai wasn't sure how many days she had been a captive. It didn't matter.

The first day, they drove for several hours. When they stopped, Walt and Mel pulled Mai out of the camper and carried her into a cabin. Walt chained her to a metal ring in a concrete wall in a back bedroom. That first night was the worse. Mel and Walt took turns at her, and Gladys watched. Eventually, she experienced nothing when Walt mauled her or ejaculated on her stomach or butt. Most times he didn't get hard enough to penetrate, her and he came so quickly, he didn't have the time to beat her.

Mel was different. He touched her until he was fully aroused. He would have hurt her had he raped her, but he didn't. He said he wanted her to enjoy the sex, to get aroused and cum with him. Her passive acceptance deflated his desire. Unlike Walt, he didn't hit her, and, he didn't try to make her perform oral sex. For a brutal killer, Mel acted almost like a gentleman with her. Eventually, Walt would tire of her, and he would kill her, but for now, she was alive, which meant the possibility of escape or rescue. Mai vowed, if she survived, she would kill Walt by her own hand. Somehow, Mel was different. She almost felt sorry for him.

~*~

Ranger Tsinnie spent Wednesday night in a local hospital. Malcolm Halah was treated in the same hospital and then transported to the Wayne County jail by a pair of Beaver County deputies. Hunter spoke on the phone with Sheriff Davenport. He was relieved to learn that his investigator was safe, and the suspect in a multiple-murder case was under arrest. However, he wondered why Hunter wasn't fishing as ordered. Davenport asked that Hunter report to his office at eight sharp on Friday.

Hunter and Tsinnie drove to Loa on Thursday morning. The plan was to talk to Mel Halah or to sit in on his interrogation. Sheriff Davenport wouldn't have approved, but Hunter had little to lose. The trip across Beaver into Wayne County reminded Hunter of living on the southern border. On the drive, Hunter talked about the day his Uncle Joseph came to school to tell Hunter, his grandfather Sam and his father had been killed in a traffic accident on Highway 163, just out of Kayenta, Arizona.

It was 1998. Hunter was sixteen and for a time, he hoped he might follow in his grandfather's footsteps to become a singer or at least a drummer. There was a time when his father had hoped the same, but booze and drugs changed his dreams. Hunter's father came back from the first Gulf War a broken man. He farmed and raised sheep during the week and drove Hunter's grandfather to ceremonies and pow wows. The police report said Jacob Táchii'nii must have fallen asleep. His truck crossed the road and hit a tree. Hunter accepted the police report and his uncle's explanation.

"Sometimes, we cannot be the man our families want us to be," said Tsinnie. "We can't even be the man we want to be. Your father gave service to the country. He raised a fine son, and I am guessing your brother and sister are the pride of their mother. If I had a son, I could only hope he would be as good a man as you."

"Thank you, Uncle. I am honored by your words. I only wish we had found Agent Yázhí."

"I believe we will find her. The key is Mel."

~*~

Mormons settled the town of Loa in 1876. Franklin Young, who had served on a mission in Hawaii, named the city. Loa means high, large, and powerful in Hawaiian. The settlement, at 7,045 feet above sea level, is one of the highest county seats in Utah. The town has a population of 514. In addition to the county courthouse and jail, there is an LDS Tabernacle, and a museum operated by the Daughters of the Utah Pioneers. The town has two motels, and the country cafe for breakfast and lunch. For dinner out, most folks go to Torrey.

Tsinnie and Hunter parked behind the courthouse building and entered by the back entrance. Deputy Blake Young sat at the front desk with one sleepy eye on the door to the jail.

"Blake, this is Ranger Custer Tsinnie. He is working the Horseshoe Canyon case. He took a bullet from our newest resident, and now, he would like some time to talk to the prisoner. Will that be okay?"

"The sheriff said you'd be in. You are not to talk to the prisoner."

"Blake—"

The deputy put up his hand. "Sheriff Davenport said nothing about the Feds. It's their case, really. If Ranger Tsinnie wants to talk to his prisoner, I don't see why not? But you should stay in one of the other rooms."

"How about the observation room? You and I could sit in the observation room while Ranger Tsinnie does his thing."

"What the hell, the chief is at lunch. That gives us an hour at least. I'd like to hear what this a-hole has to say."

Deputy Young entered the cell and took Mel to an interrogation room. He chained Mel to a metal table that was bolted to the floor. Tsinnie entered and sat opposite Mel.

"Do you know who I am?" Tsinnie asked in a low, somber voice.

"Park Service."

"Yes, that's right. I have some questions I'd like to ask."

"I'm not talking. I want a lawyer."

"These aren't questions related to your case."

"Bullshit, it doesn't matter. I ain't talking."

"I understand you are part Navajo."

"My great grandfather was Near-To-Water Clan."

"Tó'áhani. I am Honágháahnii–One-Walks-Around. We are related."

"That's not what the tribal elders decided. One-eighth wasn't enough."

"I am sorry for that, Nephew. Where did you grow up?"

"St. George."

"And how are you related to Wallace Fremont?"

"Walt is my brother, my half-brother. His father and my mother."

"Were they married?"

"It doesn't matter. His father was my father. We are brothers."

"I never questioned that, it is just Halah is a Navajo name, but your mother wasn't Navajo."

"Mormon. As white as they come."

"And, what was her name?"

"I ain't saying."

"It doesn't matter. We have your fingerprints. Was it your idea to steal artifacts or Walt's?"

"Who says we stole any artifacts?"

"The lance you killed officer Hitchens with. Was that a real antique or something you made?"

"I have no idea what you are talking about."

"A National Park Service Ranger named Cal Hitchens was killed using a native lance with a stone or obsidian blade. I'm wondering was that a real Fremont Lance or something Walt made?"

"You are wasting your time."

"It's my time. I understand Ranger Hitchens had occasion to warn Walt about poaching. The word is he beat the shit out of Walt."

"Walt did nothing wrong. That old man had it out for Walt."

"So, you did know him?"

"What if I did?"

"That makes his murder premeditated, you had a motive. You had the lance. I'm just wondering if a fake lance is worth dying over."

"It wasn't like that."

"Do you like to fish?"

"What? Sure."

"How about hunting? Do you like hunting?"

"Yes, again."

"Where do you usually go? Up north, or do you have a place down here?"

"North is better, but I shot a four-pointer south of Teasdale."

"Where will I find Walt?"

"You won't."

"I'm guessing when he learns about you being in jail, and Gladys being dead, he'll show himself again. Sooner or later, he'll go back to Horseshoe Canyon. To his cache."

"He's smarter than that."

"I don't think so. The smart one is in jail. All that is left of your artifacts business is Walt and a few boxes of arrowheads. Walt will go back to what he knows, and I'll catch him."

There was a knock on the door. Tsinnie stepped out.

"They just called from Beaver," said Hunter. "Gladys had a book of matches from Pine Mountain Cabins in Teasdale. I thought you might want to ask Mel about Teasdale, again?"

"How far is Teasdale?"

"Fourteen miles. Maybe we should go have a look."

"Nephew, for the last couple of days, you and I have been acting like cowboys."

"So?"

"Maybe we should start acting like Indians. Do a little scouting first?"

"What do you propose? More missionaries?"

"Not exactly, I'll make some calls. But first I have a couple more questions for Mel."

Tsinnie returned to the interrogation room. He sat quietly for a moment.

"So, what now?" asked Mel.

"Did you ever stay at the Capitol Reef Resort?"

"What."

"It's this place with chuck wagons and tee pees for rooms. I'm thinking of spending the night. They have a pool."

"What am I, a travel agent?"

"You and Walt are big spenders. I thought you might have stayed there. How about in Teasdale? Isn't there a motel there or a cabin?"

Mel flinched but said nothing more.

Tsinnie, wished Mel, "good luck."

Tsinnie spent the next hour on his phone. Hunter and Blake moved Mel back to his cell. He would be moved to a federal jail later in the week. Until then he'd have to listen to Sheriff Davenport's stories about politics and the Mormon pioneers.

~*~

They waited in Teasdale in the LDS church parking lot. The church was a block south on West 125th South. Pine Mountain cabins were visible a block west of the church.

It was two hours before a new Jeep pulled up, followed by a Datsun sedan and a Chevy half-ton truck. The driver of the Datsun was Sam Lapahie. In the Chevy was Ben Nabahe. The couple in the Jeep were introduced as Tom and Betty Williams from the park service. They were a married couple who worked the information desk in Capitol Reef.

The group stood around the Jeep. Hunter let Tsinnie lay out the plan. "We believe it is possible Agent Yázhí is being held in one of the cabins. Tom and Betty are going to the office to rent a cabin. Their job is to identify the cabin where Mai Yázhí is being held. If possible, they are to rent a cabin on either side. They will carry my duffle into their rental, wait a few minutes, and then leave the cabins. Go in and get out. Don't even look at the other cabins."

"When we are certain about the cabin, we will wait until dark and then go in on foot. Everyone will wear a vest. We will wait until after midnight. Hunter will go in first. I'll follow. You two will guard the front and rear. Any questions?"

"What if there is no car or truck at the cabins?"

"Let's take one step at a time. Tom, you and Betty need to go in for a look-see."

It was forty minutes before Tom and Betty returned to the church parking lot. The motel owner put them in Cabin Four. He explained he had seven cabins, but only one with two bedrooms, Cabin

Seven. He mentioned it was rented by two couples staying for a week. Cabin Four was in the middle of the row of cabins. Cabin Seven was behind the rest.

"That's the good news," said Tom.

"What's the problem?" Hunter asked.

"There's no car at Cabin Seven."

"Could you see anything? Any movement?"

"It's locked up tight."

"He could be grocery shopping or…"

"He could be gone."

"And, her with him."

"We have to check, and now is the moment."

"We could wait for him to return and take him outside the cabin."

"That makes sense. It is safer."

"Alice Sweetwater died because I wasted a day waiting for Walt to show up."

"Let's suit up. Tom, you and Betty wait here. Call me if anyone heads toward the cabins. We will follow the plan. Hunter goes in through the front door. Ben and Sam will stand guard."

"I wonder if the owner will give me the key to Cabin Seven?" said Hunter.

"He'll ask for a warrant," said Tsinnie.

"I could get one in a couple of hours, but then it will become a county enterprise."

"Try to get a key. If you can't, I'll pay for the door."

Hunter convinced the owner to give him a key to Cabin Seven. The men gathered in Cabin Four. From the back window, they could see Cabin Seven. They agreed to wait until it was dark before making any move. At nine o'clock, a light came on in the cabin. The four men were uncertain what to do.

"He must have parked the car somewhere else. We should go in now," said Tsinnie.

"Why not wait until after midnight? Let him go to sleep," said Ben Nabahe. The four men looked at each other knowing what was unsaid.

Ben Nabahe spent most of his life saying yes to others and doing what he was told. His mother died giving birth to Ben. He was raised by the women in his grandmother's house, and by the women in his tribe. Ben's father was a rodeo rider and a gambler. He taught Ben to love horses, and he taught him to drink. Ben cherished the one and hated his father for the other.

In school, Ben was an indifferent student, but he did what he was told, and he got results. He tried to live in the traditional ways. He developed into a horseman, and a crack rifle shot and hunter. Like his father, Ben liked living in the white world. A certain type of white woman found a handsome, strong Indian man like him irresistible. Likewise, he found such easy and wild women hard to resist. By the time he was twenty-three, he didn't belong in his clan, and he didn't belong in the white Mormon world of southern Utah. Fortunately, he got to talking to a tribal policeman at a rodeo in Shiprock. The officer said that he, too had been wild and spinning out of the Diné, but the police academy changed that. He learned discipline, and he found a way to help his people. Ben signed up the next day.

Tom Williams drove up while they were waiting. He was followed by a Chrysler 300. Tom used his key to enter the cabin. He was followed by an older man wearing jeans and a shooting vest, Sheriff Davenport.

"Sheriff, I don't understand. What are you doing here?" asked Hunter.

"The owner and I are friends. He called me after you persuaded him to give you a key to Cabin Seven. Perhaps you should introduce me to your friends."

"Ranger Tsinnie is representing the National Park Service. Officer Ben Nabahe and Sergeant Sam Lapahie are with the tribal police, and this is Tom Williams. He works for the Park Service. He is not armed, and he should leave."

"No, that will seem too unusual. He has to stay," said Davenport. "Gentlemen, I would like to speak with my deputy alone, but we are short on time, and I need some answers. Is Wallace Fremont in Cabin Seven?"

"One of the two men who checked in matched his description. We can't be sure who is inside. Someone must be in there—unless there is a light on a timer," said Tsinnie.

"Do you know if Agent Yázhí is inside?"

"We aren't sure," said Hunters.

"It sounds like you boys don't know shit."

"Gladys Fremont and Malcolm Halah were here three nights ago before they left for Gladys's house in Lyman. We know Mel is in prison because of Tsinnie, Sam, and Ben."

"Yes, and Gladys Fremont, an innocent spouse is dead."

"Sheriff, that isn't fair," said Hunter.

"Son, I don't give a shit about fair. You all are acting without the necessary authority. My authority."

"Sheriff. Walt Fremont and his brother Mel brutally raped a twenty-two-year-old college student and then left her to die in Horseshoe Canyon. The same is not going to be true for Agent Yázhí," said Hunter.

"So, what's the plan?" asked Davenport.

"We wait an hour or so until the light goes out and then when Walt is asleep, we go in."

"Why not go in now?"

"We don't have enough men or the right tools. The men going through the door will be very exposed."

"Should we call in SWAT?" asked Davenport.

"That's up to you. It is unlikely they can get here and act before dawn."

"That's too long. We need to go in the next two hours," said Sam.

"What we need are stun and flash grenades. Night vision, and two more men," said Hunter.

"What about helmets?" asked Davenport.

"Not for us," said Sam. The men laughed.

"Okay. It is nine thirty. I'll have the men and supplies here by eleven. We go in at midnight."

Sheriff Davenport was good to his word. Two deputies, Kyle Trainer and Ed Baskin, arrived with a supply of M84 flash-stun grenades. Both men had tactical training, and they had body armor and assault rifles. They would enter the cabin first, followed by Hunter. Tsinnie, Ben, and Sam. Sheriff Davenport would remain outside guarding the front.

At ten, the cabin light went out. At a quarter to midnight, Kyle Trainer was at the door with the key in the lock. Ben stood at one of the two front windows. His job was to smash the window and throw in a flash grenade. Kyle would enter the cabin the moment the grenade exploded.

On Kyle's signal, Ben pulled the pin on the grenade and then used the butt of his rifle to break one pane in the window and throw the grenade into the main room. The grenade produced a loud *bang* and a blinding flash of light. For an instant, the main room in the cabin was lit up like the sun. The flash and bang were intended to blind and disorient anyone in the main room. Kyle rushed into the room with his assault rifle leading the way. Kyle stepped right as Ed Baskin entered and stepped left. The room returned to darkness as Hunter stepped into the room. They found no one in the main room. That left the two-bedroom doors.

Anyone in the bedrooms would not have been affected by the flash from the grenade, but they would have been awakened by the bang. Kyle advanced to the door on the left. He shouted, "Police, drop your weapons, and raise your arms." He shouted into his lapel microphone, "Go, go!"

In the back behind the cabin, Sam Lapahie broke the left rear window and threw in a grenade. At the sound of the grenade, Kyle kicked in the bedroom door on his right. He was prepared to shoot anything that moved. It appeared empty. "Clear," he called.

"Go right," Ed Baskin called. Sam broke a pane in the other window and pitched in a grenade. In the blinding flash that followed he saw a figure standing in the room.

Baskin kicked in the door and shouted, "Drop your weapons." A man in his underwear stood behind the bed in the corner of the small bedroom. He had long hair and a long beard. He looked to be in his early twenties, perhaps younger. He had a rifle in his right hand held at his side.

"Drop the weapon," Haskin shouted. He pointed the assault rifle at Ralph Langwell.

"Ralph, don't be stupid. Drop your rifle," shouted Hunter.

Ralph appeared dazed. He looked at the men and his rifle. He lifted the rifle, perhaps to throw it down, perhaps to shoot at Haskin. Hunter wasn't sure. His training said shoot, but his read on the situation said different. It didn't matter. Sheriff Davenport stepped in front of Hunter and Baskin and pulled the rifle out of the boy's hand. "Ralph Langwell," he shouted. "What can you be thinking?"

A quick search of the cabin proved Ralph was alone. At first, he said nothing except he wanted a lawyer. Hunter expected to have to beat an answer out of him, especially after they found evidence that a woman had been bound to the bed in the other room. The questioning would be up to Sheriff Davenport and Hunter.

"Where's Walt Fremont?" asked Sheriff Davenport.

"He's not here," Ralph said with a smirk.

"Ralph, growing up you were such a good boy. What happened to you?" asked the Sheriff.

"I got smart."

"Yes, but the thing is, you are going to a federal prison for eight to twenty years as an accessory to kidnapping and murder. I'd hate to tell you what they do to boys like you in prison."

"You can't hold me. I've done nothing," said Ralph.

"It is a crime to resist arrest. That's why we had to break your fingers."

"What are you talking about, I didn't resist arrest?"

"Not yet, but I am certain you will unless you tell us something useful. Where is Walt? How did you get here? Why are you here?"

"I went to feed the chickens. I found Walt in the barn. He was angry. He kept talking about his brother and Gladys not coming back for him. He said he needed the ATV for one more run into the canyon. He said he had this big cache, and if I helped him, I'd get a cut."

"What did you do?"

"I couldn't do anything. You impounded my ATV."

The boy grinned like he had a secret.

"But you figured out something, didn't you?"

"I asked him why he didn't do it the Indian way?"

"Meaning?" asked Davenport.

"Horses," said Tsinnie.

"Where would he get horses?" shouted Hunter.

"Mark Campbell has a horse ranch over by that old ghost town," said Ralph.

"Giles," said Hunter.

"Yep, that's the one. He has a corral with a well, and he puts out hay. He usually has a few head on the range there. It's fenced. I figured that was close to where Walt needed to go, and Mark always needs money."

"Did it occur to you Walt might not pay for the horses?" asked Sheriff Davenport.

"Walt isn't like that. He's a decent guy."

"Did he have a woman with him? A Navajo woman?"

"No, he was alone, but I never saw his truck."

"So why are you here?"

"Walt said he had this cabin for two weeks. Said he didn't want the owner getting nosey. He said if I stayed here while he was gone, he'd pay me. Besides, there's plenty of food and TV, even the internet."

"Is there anything else you can tell us?"

"Walt looks different."

"How so?" asked Hunter

"He's shaved his head except for this slight flat top, and he was dressed like an Indian."

"What does that mean? Dressed like me," asked Hunter.

"No real old-time dress. Moccasins, white pants and shirt. He even had on a white headband. He looked like one of those Indians in the museum. Strange."

"You better pack up your things. You are going with us."

"I didn't do anything," said Ralph.

"That will be for the court to decide," said Sheriff Davenport.

 Mai Yázhí struggled to cover her eyes in the bright sun. After so many days in the dark, the light of day was like fire. Walt pulled her out of the camper. They were by a horse corral. She heard cars on a highway. The land looked like southern Utah, but she knew she could be in any of the four corners.

"I assume you can ride a horse," he said. He cut her bound hands. "Put your hands out front. We are going for a ride later. There is water in the trailer. I am going to take your gag out so you can drink. If you make a sound, I'll kill you here. She nodded. She could barely stand to look at him. He bound her hands in front of her and then removed her gag. She considered attacking him, but she was too weak and too thirsty."

"Come in here and be quiet." He dragged her into the front of a horse trailer. She lay down on a half bale of hay. "Remember, no sound." He led two horses into the trailer and then sealed it. She drank water and tried to think what she could do to help herself. *Wait and drink more water*, she thought.

~*~

Mai felt like she had been riding for days. He gave her one of Gladys's country dresses to wear, but she was naked underneath. He said it made everything easier. She no longer argued or cared. She bunched a layer of the dress under her bare bottom and kept her eyes ahead, always watching for some way to escape.

When they finally stopped. Mai wasn't sure if it was simply too dark, or they had reached the spot where he would kill her. He got down off his horse and pulled her down off her mount.

"Lie down," he commanded. He covered her in a blanket. If you must pee or shit, do it here. If you leave this spot, I'll shoot you. When I'm finished, I'll give you some water, and you can sleep. Remember, no sound.

He tied the horses to a cottonwood tree and paced off steps from the tree. He had a compass. When he returned, he had a long wooden ladder, the type the Hopi used to enter their sweat lodge. She watched him place the ladder against a cliff wall. He climbed the ladder and searched the cliff face. Eventually, he climbed down. *He has a hidey-hole so well hidden even he can't find it*, Mai thought.

Mai wasn't sure how many times he climbed the ladder and came down. At least five. Finally, he pulled a painted canvas away from the wall. In the fading light, she could just make out a hole the size of a basketball hoop. With considerable difficulty, he climbed headfirst into the hole.

This was her chance, but still, she waited. She didn't see Walt at first, only the rifle barrel. He wanted her to run. Instead, she sat up and took the opportunity to pee. She had stopped shitting two days earlier.

168

When he returned, he uncuffed her and dragged her to the ladder. "I want you to crawl into that hole and wait for me," he said. "If you make a sound or look out the cave opening, I'll kill you."

The ladder was easily thirty feet tall. What surprised her was a second ladder somehow attached to the wall. It was another twenty feet. It took all her strength to climb the ladders and crawl into the cave. Inside it was big enough for three people. She saw a smoke hole above her head. *People lived here thousands of years ago*, she thought. In a corner of the space were piles of pots and other artifacts, including lances, stone knives, and arrowheads.

He has forgotten what is in here, she thought. She found an obsidian knife. *When he sticks his head in, I'm going to slit his throat*, she thought. She waited beside the cave opening.

"We are going to have company," he called. "I'm going to leave you now. Wish me luck, because if I don't survive, neither do you." He climbed down after working at the cover for a time.

She pushed against the cover to the cave. It didn't move. It was like a metal skin over a drum. She pushed with her hands and her feet. Nothing she did moved the cover. Exhausted, she waited and listened. For the first time, she almost hoped he would return.

~*~

Pinnacle Air offered helicopter rides over Canyonlands and other scenic areas of interest. The forty-five-minute trip over Horseshoe Canyon normally cost $175 per person. For the park service, they reduced the rate and expanded the search to ninety minutes. They were searching for riders on horseback in the canyon or a truck towing a horse trailer into the area. It was Friday afternoon. Less than fifteen minutes after takeoff, they were following the green river to Horseshoe Canyon.

There were cars and hikers at the trailhead, but no horse trailer. Hunter could make out people walking along the river bottom. He saw a glimpse of the Ghosts on the Gallery Wall. Further south, past the canyon and out on the high desert plain, they saw a Chevy two-and-a-half-ton truck with a horse trailer. The trailer was parked at the end of a dirt road that branched off from Hans Fall Road. The trailer appeared empty.

They flew close in and several feet off the ground. After checking the license plate, Hunter determined it was Campbell's truck and trailer. Tsinnie pointed to horse tracks going into a dry creek.

"We should send a team in to be waiting at the Great Gallery. At his hidey-hole."

"I agree, but we can't be sure that is where he is going. We have to follow him from here."

"Should I call for an ATV?" asked Tsinnie.

"He will hear us coming. What we need to get are some horses and go in after him."

"You have a horse in Hanksville."

"Yes."

"Fly us to Hanksville, we are getting off," Tsinnie told the pilot. "I'll need to make a call."

"He's got several hours on us. That is a big head start," said Hunter.

"Not for Sam Lapahie."

They landed in a field a block away from Hunter's trailer. He went across the street to his neighbor's barn to get his horse and saddle. His neighbor Kim Wheatley was raking hay into an empty stall.

"Hunter," he said, "what's going on. Where have you been?"

"I am taking Blackie into the canyons. This nut has a woman, and he is taking her into Horseshoe."

"Is he the one from last week? The one on the news?"

"His brother."

"Is he armed?"

"A hunting rifle."

"What are you taking with you?"

"The usual, water, food, camping gear."

"I mean in terms of weapons."

"My Glock and I guess my Winchester. We didn't talk weapons; this is kind of on the fly. My partner has called in some tribal police. They'll have deer rifles."

"Tie up Blackie and come in for a minute. I might have a couple of guns for you and your partner."

Hunter had only been in Wheatley's house once before.

"I have a couple of rifles that might be an improvement on your Winchester. What is it, a Winchester 94?"

"It is a 73. It was my grandfather's."

"That belongs in a showcase."

He opened a large metal, gun locker.

"Here is a Marlin 336C, similar short barrel, great lever action, and this has a scope. I even have a saddle case. The thing I like about the Marlin is it is great in the bush and it is a 30-30. Now, this is something altogether different." He pulled out an assault rifle. "This is the Ambush 300 Blackout. It is a .30 caliber Assault Rifle with a short barrel and a scope. Given your background, this is the weapon for you."

"Do you have a saddle bag for it?"

"That and two extra magazines."

Wheatley loaned Hunter one of his duffle bags for the guns, ammo, and saddle holsters. Tsinnie was on the phone. Hunter used the time to put together camping supplies and coordinate with the sheriff's department. Sergeant Sam Lapahie and Officer Ben Nabahe arrived in a Ford truck towing a large trailer with three horses: a big bay, and two smaller mustangs. Sergeant Lapahie looked like he was going to a rodeo, wearing blue jeans, a blue cowboy shirt with a white collar, white straw hat, and cowboy boots. Out of place were his bulletproof vest and his Remington deer rifle. Ben Nabahe was as handsome as ever, and still in uniform.

They left as soon as Hunter's pony was loaded into the trailer. It took thirty-four minutes to reach Hans Fall Ranger Station. The trackers left their trailer with the ranger on duty. They had the advantage that the station was closer and an easier entrance to Horseshoe Canyon.

"Let's pack up," said Hunter.

"It will be dark soon," said Ben.

"It doesn't matter. We must follow them now," said Sam.

The four set out at a good pace with Sam Lapahie leading the way riding his bay horse. Hunter may have been named Nalje, but Sam was a true sign reader. He was a tracker; the kind of Navajo the Army used to hunt down the Apache. Sam called his horse "Big Boy," and he and Big Boy seemed as if they moved as one. The horse followed the tracks without Sam using the reins. The horse would stop, and Sam would look and then pat the horse on the side saying, "Good Boy," as if the horse was a hound dog.

Without any discussion, the four set into a pattern of speaking in Diné and English. Often when talking about their horses or the land, they used Diné words. When they talked about Walt, they talked in English. Sometimes they would use both words as if a non-native was listening.

When he was a boy, Hunter liked to assume the role of Monster Slayer, the hero twin. When he was around his older uncle, he became Born in Water, the younger twin. Around, Sam and Ben, he felt like he was once again Born in Water. They seemed to know so much more about the business of tracking. Tsinnie, on the other hand, treated Hunter like a valued nephew, but also as an equal in the business of being a law officer.

Two hours in, the sun disappeared over the cliff tops. They still had an hour or more of light, but after that, they would be riding in the dark.

"Will he stop?" Sam asked in English.

"He's a pot hunter. Most likely he will have headlamps," said Ben.

"I wish I had thought of those," said Hunter.

"Nephew," said Sam. "Big Boy can smell another horse, and he has the eyes of the coyote. We are not miners. We are not day hikers from New York. Reach out and feel your prey."

"Sam, don't be silly."

"I mean it, reach out, and seek signs of your prey."

Hunter put the reins in his teeth and reached out with both hands.

"There, Nephew, do you feel it, do you feel the force?" The three older men laughed together. Sam and Ben had played that joke on a dozen new officers.

"Very funny Obi-Wan."

"Hunter, I know they are still riding. I sense it and Big Boy senses it, too. One day, so will you. You have all the makings of Gray Wolf, Ma' iitsoh. You could be a chief, but for now, you are satisfied to be the protector of your people. I see this in you. The wolf is a great hunter, alone he is strong; but in his tribe, his pack, he is stronger."

"You honor me, Uncle, but the wolf is also feared."

"You know the story of the Navajo grandfather who told his grandson, 'There are two wolves that live inside of me. One is the bad wolf, full of greed and laziness, full of anger and jealousy and regret. The other is the good wolf, full of joy and compassion and willingness and a great love for the world. All the time, these wolves are fighting inside of me.' And, the boy says, 'Which wolf will win?' and the grandfather answered, 'the one I feed.'"

"Am I feeding both?" Hunter asked.

"What do you think?"

"I want to save Yázhí, but I want to eat Fremont's beating heart."

"Gray Wolf would want nothing less," said Sam. "We should walk the horses for a while. We are making good time, but we don't want to catch up with our prey at the wrong moment."

They had been riding at four miles an hour. They walked at something closer to two miles an hour. Using the GPS on his cellphone, Tsinnie figured they had traveled seven of the twenty-two miles they expected to ride. Tsinnie used his flashlight on the tracks. They had the advantage of a half moon.

"They are walking, too," said Sam. He pointed to a pile of horse dung. "Not very old," he said. "Maybe two hours."

"How can you tell without touching it?"

"If you want to be sure, go ahead."

"No, I just want to learn Obi-Wan."

"I've shoveled a lot of horseshit. It wasn't steaming, but it wasn't dry and hard. More than an hour, less than four."

"I'll take your word."

They walked and rode for another hour. Sam was certain they were gaining ground. When it was too dark to ride, Sam called a halt.

"I'm going to feed the horses some pellets and give them some water. Why don't you help me with the horses? Ben and Tsinnie can set up a place to sleep. It's going to be cold tonight, but we can't afford a fire. That means cold beans and sleeping together," said Sam.

"When can we start again?" asked Hunter.

"It's eleven forty. First light is around five thirty. I want to be packed and set out by four. My guess is they have reached the spot where he has his cache. Likely, he will start collecting at first light, and we can have him before any tourists get in the way."

Good to his word, Sam got them up at three thirty. They packed in silence, and before they left their camp, they put on their armored vests. Each man had the vest provided by his department. They were level II vests, capable of stopping most handgun bullets, but not the steel-jacketed military rounds.

"I'm not sure my vest will stop a rifle round," said Hunter.

"I know mine won't. Still, they look good," said Tsinnie.

"The best offense is a good defense," said Ben.

"We few, we noble few, we band of brothers," quoted Sam.

"Let's see if we can avoid being blood brothers," said Hunter.

They headed out before four in the morning. For the next hour, Sam used a narrow-beam flashlight pointed down to follow Walt and Mai's horse tracks.

As the sky grew lighter, they increased the distance between each horse, and they rode with their rifles across their saddles. They looked like the Navajos who rode the plains one hundred and fifty years earlier. Sam continued to lead, but now he and Big Boy hugged the cottonwoods and brush along the river bed. An expanse of scrub brush and red sand appeared between the cliff walls and the dry river. This was open ground that offered no shelter. Sam watched the walls as much as he watched the path in front of him. He expected an ambush. They all did.

The north side of the canyon was showing signs of daybreak. The cliff ledge took on an orange color. Hunter followed behind Sam, with Ben and Tsinnie riding trail. Sam stopped and got down off his horse, being careful to keep his body behind the horse. With his head down, he walked the horse forward.

"They stopped here," he called. "Someone lay over here. I'm guessing the woman. There are footprints to the cliff face, but the tracks are confused. He walked back and forth here, but he led the horses away. I might be wrong, but her horse is lighter going forward."

"You think she's here?"

"I don't know what to think. We must be careful. We are no longer the hunters."

Sam made a clicking sound, and the bay walked forward on its own. A bullet hit the bay in the neck and knocked Sam's cowboy hat off his head before he heard the shot. Big Boy took a step forward and collapsed, taking Sam in the saddle with him.

Bullets dug into the sand behind Sam's head. A second bullet drove through the big bay's chest. The horse jerked and lay still.

"I'm going to kill that fucker," said Sam.

Hunter crawled up behind Sam using the horse's hind quarter as cover. He used the scope on the Ambush 300 to try to find Fremont.

"That last shot was pretty level. I don't think he is very high," said Hunter.

"He's not on the ridge," said Sam.

"He's in a tree or on top of those boulders by the Ghost Wall?"

178

"There is only one way to find out. Ben," Sam called, "Hunter is going to lay down covering fire. I want you to go over to those Cottonwoods, and hunt for our sniper. Try to stay alive."

"What are you going to do?"

"Once you are in place, I'm going to make a run for those cottonwoods up there. The thing is, I have to pull my rifle out from under Big Boy, and I am not sure I can manage."

"Take my gun." Hunter pushed the assault rifle into Sam's hand. "I have another on my saddle. Here is an extra clip. I'll be back in a minute." He crawled away and quickly returned with his grandfather's Winchester 73.

"Okay, on three, you fire at the middle branches in that cottonwood, and I'll fire along the top of the boulder. One, two, three." Together they sat up and laid down fire into the trees and boulders in front of them. At the same time, Ben ran across the riverbed to the south side of the canyon, and Tsinnie crawled up behind Hunter. Even as they were firing, several bullets zipped by or hit the dead horse.

Sam started singing in a low voice. He was praying for Big Boy. In normal times, he would have spread pollen and butchered the horse for meat. Now he sang to drive away evil spirits. Navajos did not like being around dead things.

"I think he is on top of those boulders," Ben called. "Cover me. I'm going to run to that rock about twenty feet ahead. Ready, now." Sam lay down a burst from the Ambush 300, and Hunter got off three quick shots. Ben half stood and ran forward to a boulder. He was still exposed when a shot rang out. It cut across the boulder sending rock fragments into Ben's handsome face. He dropped down behind the rock and didn't move.

"What do you want to do?" Sam asked. He sounded different.

"I could try to ride to the Gallery Wall."

"If he didn't kill you, he'd kill your pony. Nothing is worth that," said Sam, with emotion in his voice.

"We can call in backup, but it will take time."

"He could leave, and we'd never know."

"We should have sent a second team in from the main trail head. Created a pincher."

"We need to do that now, and make sure no one—no civilians—come into the canyon. I have been stupid," said Sam.

"I'll call for backup and get things moving," said Hunter. "Whatever happens, I want Tsinnie to stay back. Someone needs to survive this, and make sure he doesn't get away."

"Agreed."

Hunter crawled back to Tsinnie. He called for backup and made sure the rangers were told to keep hikers out of the canyon. Tsinnie stood with the horses. His face was grim and determined.

"Uncle, I have fucked up."

"Nephew, we accepted the danger."

"If it goes bad for us, I want you to take the horses and ride back out of the canyon. It is important to me that one of us can continue the search for Mai. If she is alive, we must save her."

"Nephew, what we need is help from above."

"Help from the gods?"

"No, we need a rifleman, a sniper on the ridge above us."

"Should I call the helicopter and see if he can put a man up there?"

"We don't have the time. You and I should try. Sam and Ben can keep him busy from here."

"I think Ben may have been hit."

"He's playing opossum."

"I'm not sure."

"I am. Let me talk to Sam."

Tsinnie crawled to Sam. They talked for several minutes. Sam then called to Ben, telling him to hold tight.

Back at the horses, Tsinnie took a coil of rope and a water bottle from his saddle bag. Then pulled the Marlin out of its case and put it over his shoulder on his back.

"Let's go, Nephew." He led Hunter back through the cottonwoods until they were out of sight and close to the wall. "We have to find a way up."

"I'm not a climber."

"Neither am I, but we are Diné. Put your hand on the wall, touch it. Use your fingers to find the first step up."

"Tsinnie, this is nuts."

"Do as I say. Touch the wall and find a hole the ancients used to climb to the top. I am sure there is a path if only we can find the first step."

"What if it is above us?"

"Open your eyes and look. There. That hole above your head. It is a handhold. There are three or four above that. Do you see?" asked Tsinnie.

"Give me a boost," said Hunter.

Tsinnie gave Hunter the coil of rope, which he attached to his backpack. Tsinnie used a handhold to push Hunter up until he had a foot in a crack and his right hand in one of the holes above. Hunter did not look down. He didn't like heights, and he had no idea how he would get back down. He took the next step pulling himself up some four feet. There were more foot-and handholds above.

After fifteen minutes of climbing, Hunter was three-quarters of the way to the top of the ridge above the ghosts. In the morning light, he had an excellent view of the Gallery wall. For a moment, he clung to the cliff face and enjoyed the beauty of the ancient symbols made by the first people to live in these canyons. The painted figures glowed red in the morning light. They danced and hunted deer once again. In his mind, Hunter traced a line from the Gallery to Sam and Ben. The stand of cottonwood trees ended before the large group of boulders. There was an open space, perhaps—one hundred feet—between the boulder and the wall.

From above, Hunter had a better understanding of where they were in the canyon. The boulders were the ones where he found Alice Sweetwater. Hunter scanned the top of the boulders again. A wooden ladder was sticking out of the entrance to Walt's cave.

Hunter wanted to get to the ridge, but there didn't seem to be any steps above him. Instead, the holes moved sideways toward a narrow ledge above the Great Galley. Hunter remembered there was a ledge, perhaps a foot wide, some sixty feet above the paintings. The ledge spanned most of the Gallery. There were cracks and caves, a line of ancient dwellings below the ridge. Looking at the ledge, he remembered that people were not allowed to explore the ridge or the caves. Too narrow, too fragile, too dangerous. No place for a man who was afraid of heights. But a perfect place for a sniper.

Hunter moved hand-over-hand, foot-by-foot across the cliff face until his right foot was on the ledge. The boulders were almost directly below him. He searched with his fingers for a handhold; something that would support him on the ledge. There were cracks, but no carved holes. Hunter knew that mountain climbers wedged their fingers into cracks as they climbed. He forced his fingers into a space and then dragged himself across until only his toes were on the rock ledge, and his heels were hanging out into space.

Hunter inched his way along the wall until he came to a wider section of ledge. Carefully, Hunter lowered himself to his knees until he could crawl along the ledge on his hands and knees. Hunter saw that he might be able to cross another hundred feet. However, that would take him farther from the boulders. What he needed was to get into a shooting position where he could make a shot without being exposed. Where he was, he would be dead the moment Fremont realized he was above him on the wall.

Hunter stood, reversed his position, and crawled another foot until he came to a large cave opening. Inside, it was dark and cool. A perfect spot for rattlesnakes and scorpions. Hunter pulled the Marlin off his back. He used the butt of the rifle to poke inside the cave. He pulled out a penlight from his ammo vest. He looked in the cave. It seemed free of snakes or any other danger. Hunter stood and then backed his way into the cave. Below him, Fremont was using the boulders and the top of the cave entrance like a tank. He'd come out the top, take a shot and then duck down under the protection of the boulders just like the turret of a tank.

Hunter used the scope on the Marlin to focus on the boulders. Walt came up for a look and then dropped back down. Hunter had found his prey, but what about Agent Yázhí? If she was with Walt, then any shot had to be immediately fatal.

Hunter settled down and sighted on the opening to the cave in the boulders. Hunter tested the air. No wind. A one-hundred-yard shot. Not far. An easy shot. He knew he could kill Walt with one shot, but he wanted to take Walt alive.

Tsinnie had expected this situation. He told Hunter to signal when he was ready. To give out an owl hoot if he had Walt in sight, or to give a coyote bark if he couldn't take a shot. Hunter had to keep Walt from shooting. With Walt pinned down, Sam and Ben would advance until they could cover Walt's position.

Hunter sighted the opening of the cave in the boulders and gave out a loud and realistic owl hoot. Walt immediately stuck his head out the cave. Hunter placed a bullet into the rock right in front of Walt. Chips of rock peppered Walt's face. Walt ducked down and then came back up with his rifle. Hunter placed another bullet in the same place, and then one to Walt's left side. Walt dropped down and didn't come back up. Hunter gave out his owl call again.

Sam and Ben started to move up on the wall. Walt stuck his head out again with his rifle. Hunter placed a shot in front of him. This time, Walt didn't drop down. Instead, he raised his rifle. Hunter's bullet shattered the rifle stock. Walt dropped the shattered weapon and looked up. He must have realized that the bullet came from above. He put his hand above his eyes. He searched the Ghost Wall. Hunter pulled back into his cave and counted to ten.

Hunter peeked back out. He could see Walt's head just below the top of the cave. Sam moved through the cottonwoods with Ben trailing behind. Watching their advance, Hunter realized Sam and Ben didn't know about the second cave entrance in the boulders. From that window, Fremont might be able to shoot Sam or Ben. Hunter got on his radio and called to Tsinnie, explaining the situation. Tsinnie said he'd take care of letting Sam know. While they were on the radio, Walt popped his head out with a pistol in his right hand. Hunter screamed into the radio, "Drop." He grabbed the Marlin and sighted on the boulders. When he had Walt in the crosshairs he fired, hoping to hit him in his shoulder. The bullet exploded on the side of Walt's head and shoulder. He dropped below the cave opening.

Sam ran at the boulders with his rifle ready. Ben had his rifle over his shoulder. He had a pistol in his right hand. Tsinnie stayed back from the others in the cottonwoods with a rifle.

Sam called on his radio, "Nice work Nephew. Now, all we have to do is get him out."

"Should I come down?"

"Do you think you can?"

"Honestly, I'm not sure. I might need a rescue."

"You should stay where you are. If he comes out again or gets away from us, you will have one shot. After that, I'll personally get you down."

"Good enough, Uncle. Be careful of the window on the side."

"Ben is standing by it. It is covered, but he found it."

"Uncle, I see movement at the opening."

Sam said something and pointed to Ben. Ben aimed his pistol at the top of the boulders. Sam climbed up onto a boulder right below the top. He crouched with his rifle at the ready. Hunter heard him call to Fremont. The words weren't clear, but his tone was pure police command voice.

Walt raised an arm above the cave opening.

"I'm shot," he called.

"Come out, and show us both your arms," said Sam.

"I can't. One is busted."

"Come out slowly," shouted Sam.

Hunter put the scope's crosshair on the cave opening.

Walt came up with one hand in the air. He must be on a ladder, thought Hunter.

Sam stood up and pointed his rifle at Walt.

Walt came up another step with his left hand in the air, and his right hand at his side. Hunter was certain he hit Walt in the left shoulder, not the right. Walt came out another step. When his right hand was clear, he raised his arm and hand. He had something in his hand. He pulled back his arm to throw. Hunter sighted on the arm. Before he could shoot, Ben shot Walt in the chest. Once again, he dropped out of sight.

Speaking in Diné, Sam asked Ben, "What the fuck?"

Ben replied. "The police manual says, if your assailant comes at you with a knife, use your gun. That was a stone knife."

"We need to make sure if he is dead."

"He will be. I shot to kill."

"We need to get him out and see if the girl is down there."

They scrambled up to the cave opening and used their flashlights to check on Walt. They were both surprised that he was alive. With Ben covering him, Sam pointed his pistol at Walt and climbed down the wooden ladder, a step at a time. Sam realized there was a second ladder behind the first.

Once he was down, he checked for Agent Yázhí. She wasn't in the cave. Next, he checked Walt's wounds. His shoulder was bleeding, and the red stain on his chest was spreading. Sam took off his backpack and grabbed a field dressing and applied it to Walt's chest.

The pot thief opened his eyes. He coughed. There was blood on his lips. "Daash yinílyé?" Walt asked.

"I am Sergeant Sam Lapahie with the tribal police. I am Tó'áhani born for Honágháahnii. My cheii was Ta'neeszahnii, my nali was Dziłtł'ahnii."

"Mountain Cove Clan," said Walt, his speech halting.

"Where is Agent Yázhí?"

"She is with the ghosts," He said with a bloody smile.

"Are you saying she is dead?"

"She is alive, but you will never find her without me, so you better get me help." He coughed more blood.

"You will not leave here alive unless you tell me where I can find Mai Yázhí. Do this to free your spirit."

"Little flower. She never told me. All the time I was deflowering her."

"Tell me where she is!"

"She is among the Ghosts—the ancient ones."

Walt tried to stab Sam with an obsidian knife.

Sam grabbed his hand, but not before Walt pushed the knife into Sam's vest. Sam felt the blade and pushed back. Sam reached for his own belt knife, a steel blade with an antler horn for a handle. He thrust the blade into Walt's stomach and drove it up into his heart.

When he was a boy, Sam would ride into the sections of the Canyonlands called the Needles, Devils Kitchen, and the Maze. These were remote sites in the park that few ever see except on horseback. Sam would spend a week at a time living off the land and drinking in his people's history. For Sam, the needle was a row of spires all red and tan, red and tan marking off centuries. On these trips, he would take a rifle, bedroll, water bag, and some jerky. Most important of all was his hunting knife. His belt knife.

Sam had a folding buck knife that one of his uncles gave him on his twelfth birthday. He also had a straight blade knife his grandfather gave him. Grandfather Joe Lapahie claimed the antler bone handle came from a buck his father, Red Shoulder, had killed using a bow and arrow. In his father's family, the story of Red Shoulder was a warrior's story. One of Red Shoulder's grandfathers was an Apache Navaho. Even as a boy, the family saw Red Shoulder as more Apache than Diné. When Red Shoulder was still a boy, he brought a buck down with one arrow. The antler knife was made for Red Shoulder by the man at the trading post. The blade was forged German steel. Grandpa Joe said Red Shoulder used the knife when he fought the Mormons and the Army. Sam had carried the knife ever since he was a boy. Now it was sticking out of Walt Fremont's chest.

"Sam, it's Ben. Are you living?"

"Barely. This da'alzhin stuck me with a stone knife. I think my vest stopped most of the blade, but I'm bleeding."

"What about the perp?"

"He's history, and I need to get out of here."

Sam pushed away from the body without touching the corpse. Even though he was a police officer and had seen his share of death, he feared the evil associated with the dead, and he wanted to free himself of his enemy and his evil spirit as soon as possible.

"Help me up," Sam called.

He stood on the third step of the ladder and reached out for Ben. His side burned with pain. Out of the cave, Sam sat on the top of the boulder while Ben treated his knife wound. The hole in Sam's side seeped blood, but a pressure bandage helped stop the flow.

"You are lucky. Your vest did very little to stop the blade. It was one of those ammo clips for that assault rifle. The blade broke on the clip."

"Where are Hunter and Tsinnie?"

"Hunter is still up on the ledge." Ben pointed up. Hunter was half out of his cave, and on the ledge waving at the two men. "Tsinnie is looking for some way to get Hunter down."

"What about those ladders," said Sam. "There are two. One must be thirty feet tall, and the other is at least twenty feet. I remember this TV show where these explorers use a series of ladders on a wall to climb up to this bat cave."

"Why would anyone want to go into a bat cave?"

"That isn't the point. Hunter has a rope. He might be able to haul one of the ladders up the cliff face and secure it so that he can climb down to the second ladder."

"It might work."

"It's worth a try. Call Tsinnie."

With Tsinnie's help, they pulled out the long ladders and carried them over to the wall below Hunter. It was agreed they would leave Walt's body for the crime scene people. They still had to find Mai Yázhí.

Tsinnie called his boss in the Park Service, and Ben called his boss and Sheriff Davenport. The cave that Hunter had used was near the center of the Great Gallery. It was possible that a ladder might reach, but Ben and Tsinnie were concerned for the primitive art. The lowest part of the ledge was just beyond the cutout in the wall that had the paintings people called the *Holy Ghost*. Centuries earlier, a large section of wall had broken away from the face, taking the existing ancient art with it. The new ghost paintings were less than one thousand years old. The painting consisted of seven figures: two small, and four larger figures painted in a dull brown red. In between two of the larger people was the ghost. It was a size-and-a-half taller and larger than the others and painted with a different lighter red. What most people remembered was the body had no arms or legs, and a skull-like head with circle eyes; many had designs painted inside the body of the figure.

South of the Holy Ghost was another wall, this one without paintings. Tsinnie found a good spot to position the first ladder. It was just a few feet from the ledge. They were talking about how to use the second ladder when Sam pointed out something unusual. Both ladders were constructed using logs for the rails and rungs. However, rather than tying the rung to the rail, Fremont had used nails, screws, and bolts. They were sturdy.

"Look at these rungs," said Sam, pointing to the third rung from the top. "There is a groove in the middle of the rung. There is a similar groove on the third rung from the bottom."

"He hung them from a hook in his garage," offered Ben.

"You wouldn't get a groove like that hanging in a garage. They had a weight applied," said Tsinnie.

"The cliff people used ladders like this to get in and out of their holes in the walls. They also used them to climb walls."

"That is what we are doing."

"Sure, but if the ladder wasn't long enough, what did they do?"

"They cut steps and foot holes."

"Like those," Tsinnie pointed to holes in the cliff wall, including those used by Hunter.

"Mountain climbers don't cut steps or foot holes any longer. They pound these wedges and hooks into the wall. What if Walt found a cave on one of these walls? A cave too high for one ladder. A cave with foot holes. A big man like Walt wouldn't want to use foot holes forever. Sooner or later, he'd fall. He figured out a way to anchor a series of ladders."

"You think that's why he had two ladders."

"We should get Hunter down. He is the only one small enough and fit enough to do any climbing."

"Should he check the caves on the ledge above the Gallery?"

"He was in the last large cave, but he can check."

It took them an hour to help Hunter down. Back on solid earth, he drank a quart of water and ate an energy bar. While Hunter finished a second granola bar, the men explained their plan to search the walls higher up for another hidey-hole. Hunter didn't mention his fear of heights. He only had two thoughts: Mai Yázhí and Walt Fremont. Surprisingly, he wanted to check on Fremont first. It didn't matter that Tsinnie and Sam assured him Fremont was dead. He had to be sure.

Hunter knew he was wasting valuable time checking on Fremont, but he needed closure. He needed the certainty and satisfaction that Walt Fremont was dead. Had he been alone, he would have been tempted to eat the man's heart. However, the dead body gave him no joy, no elation. He was expecting to feel relieved, but Yázhí was still a prisoner, and Walt seemed like he was at peace.

Tsinnie helped Hunter down from the boulders.

"How do you feel, Nephew?"

"Not as I expected. He was an evil man, and we stopped him, but the taste in my mouth is bitter."

"Monster Slayer had to kill the monsters because they threatened the people, but he felt no joy in his deeds. Come, we have more important work to do."

They walked back to Ben and Sam. Sam was laying against a rock using his binoculars.

"I don't see anything," said Sam, handing the binoculars to Ben.

"What should I be looking for?" asked Ben.

"Remember how Walt camouflaged the entry to his cave in the boulders? If there is a hidey-hole in one of these walls, it's likely he's done the same. We'll have to scan the walls for anything unusual."

"Like hooks," said Tsinnie. "If we find a hook, we have a chance."

"Do we go back to the Ghost Wall?"

"We may have to, but let's start here. If we find nothing we will check the wall on the other side of the Gallery. He'd want a spot that wasn't as trafficked as the Great Gallery."

"How soon will the crime scene people arrive?"

"That depends on my boss and Sheriff Davenport," said Tsinnie. "My guess is we have another two or three hours before someone can remove the body."

"If you ask me, I think we will need a ceremony here to rid the wall of Walt's evil spirit," said Sam.

"That will take a nine-day sing," commented Ben.

"The evil will never be gone if we don't find Mai," said Hunter.

"The ghosts won't let her die—not here," said Tsinnie.

"I may have something," said Ben. "Grab the ladders and follow me."

He walked slowly along the wall, touching the sandstone as he went. Every other step, he'd look up to find the spot, again.

"Look up there." He pointed to a spot twenty feet about their heads. "What is that?"

"It is just an old, rusty nail."

"It's too big for a nail. It's more like a spike."

"I don't see anything above it."

"And you won't. This guy was smarter than we believed, and he understood about the old ways. Sometimes, rather than cut steps or use a whole ladder, the Pueblo people would nail ladder rungs right to the wall. That spike is meant to look like something old. But in the binoculars, it looks like it was painted, and now the paint is wearing off. I think it is a steel spike."

"Let's try the ladders," said Tsinnie.

They put the longer ladder against the wall. The top of the ladder was a foot below the spike. Hunter climbed to the top and then hoisted the second ladder until the ladder was leaning against the wall with the left side of the third rung resting on the spike.

"Try moving the ladder back and forth."

Hunter moved the ladder to his right. Before he could stop it, it toppled sideways, and fell to the ground, barely missing Ben.

"This isn't the spot. It's just an old spike," said Ben.

"You must try again," said Tsinnie.

"Nephew," called Sam.

"The spike has to sit in the center of the rung, in that groove. My guess is, as hard as this will be, the top rung must be in the right spot before the bottom rung is lowered. Try lifting the ladder higher than you need, and then slowly put the top against the wall and lower the ladder until the rung is on the center."

"I may not be tall enough."

"I know you can."

It took three more tries, but Hunter finally got the ladder on the rung in such a way that it didn't move sideways. Hunter was exhausted. Looking down made his head swirl. Carefully, he reached for a rung on the second ladder and stepped up. There were two rungs to go on the first ladder, but as a child, Hunter was taught never to step on or trust the top rung. He pulled himself up with his hands and until he had a foot on the bottom rung of the second ladder. On the next step up, it seemed like he and the ladder might easily be pulled off the wall if he leaned back any space at all.

He hugged the wall and started to climb. Rather quickly, he stood on the second-to-the-last rung at the top and used cracks in the wall to keep him in position. With his right hand and arm, he inched along the wall face, hoping to find a piece of canvas or some covering. He climbed one rung higher and tried again. Twice he nearly fell. There was nothing.

"Come down Nephew," Sam called. "We will keep looking."

"This has to be right," he called. "There is something I am missing. What was that?" cried Hunter.

"What?"

"Quiet, be quiet. I thought I heard a drum."

"It is the ghosts, they are chanting," called Sam.

"Be quiet."

They listened for several minutes, hearing the wind through the leaves and the cry of a hawk. Then a faint thump.

"There it is," said Hunter.

"I heard it too. Very faint."

"It is below me."

Hunter started down the ladder. Half way down, he slipped in his haste and grabbed at the rung and the rock face. He finally stopped his descent using his hands as much as his feet. Leaning into the wall, he regained his breath and his courage. Once again, he heard the beat of a drum. *Thump, Thump. Thump.* It was close, but it sounded higher up the wall.

Hunter climbed back up a step. The thump was louder. He felt the wall on either side of the ladder and between the rungs. Two steps up, he touched a piece of painted canvas. Immediately, he realized the ladder was too high on the spikes. To get at the cave entrance, he needed the top of the second ladder to be moved down two or three feet.

He pulled at the canvas. It barely moved. Exploring around the edges, he found what appeared to be fasteners; small hooks that held the canvas tight and in place. With some effort, he managed to release one end of the canvas. Excited, he leaned into the opening. A stone-age knife barely missed cutting his forehead. Jumping back, he nearly fell, screaming, "Sweet Jesus."

"Hunter is that you?" Mai called.

"Mai, you're alive. Oh, my God. She's alive," he called to the others. The men on the ground began to cheer.

"Mai, I have the ladder too high. Look out and tell me if you can crawl between the rungs. Otherwise, I'll move the ladder. Do you need water? When did you last eat? Should I call in the medi-evac?"

"Hunter, slow down. Do you have any extra clothes?"

"I have jeans and a T-shirt."

"Get them for me. I'll be all right." Hunter was surprised by how calm Mai sounded. The cop in her had taken over.

Hunter went back down onto the first ladder. He called down to Tsinnie telling him what he wanted from his saddlebags. Then he moved the second ladder, dropping it down two rungs until the top of the ladder was just at the cave entrance. As much as he hated Walt Fremont, he had to admire his craftsmanship.

Mai Yázhí was down on the ground and eating an energy bar when the first group of officials arrived. Tsinnie and Sam sat with Mai, not saying anything or asking questions. They simply sat with her, offering her their presence and understanding. She was wrapped in a blanket dressed in Hunter's jeans and a T-shirt. On her feet, she had Hunter's red moccasins. They were big, but not too big. Looking at Yázhí, you would not have guessed she endured six days of deprivation and torture from two sadistic killers.

Hunter and Ben brought up the horses and supplies. They expected Sam and Tsinnie would go out with Yázhí; go out with the medical team on an ATV. Instead, they planned to ride out the way they had come in. Hunter managed to get the saddle and gun off Big Boy. The two men stood for a long silent moment praying for the horse.

"Uncle, should we bury him or butcher him?"

"Sam should decide. I'm guessing the park service won't want the body buried, and there will be too many cameras."

"Let's have the park service take the carcass, and I'll bury the hide under a juniper tree like in old times," said Sam, when he was asked.

Agent Yázhí asked if she could have a moment alone with Hunter before she went with the medical team. Sam was already sitting rather uncomfortably in one of the four-wheel vehicles.

"Hunter, I just wanted to say thank you. Tsinnie told me about Gladys and Mel and your gun battle with Walt. I owe my life to you."

"I got you captured. I fucked up."

"You and I know that isn't true. I was too anxious, too impulsive. I put both of us in danger."

"I'm just glad you are alive; I can't imagine. . ."

"Please, we can talk about that later. Right now, all I want to do is see my son and have a long bath. After that, I'll need to cleanse myself of his evil. I'll need a sweat ceremony. I'm hoping you and others will join me. You don't have to decide now. Talk together."

"Say hello to Ahote for me."

"How…"

"I stopped to make sure your mother was all right. Tsinnie and I stopped."

"How was my mother, and Ahote?"

"She's a rock. She and Tsinnie seem to hit it off. Ahote was all smiles and laughter, but then he was a bit fussy. I think he misses you."

"You visited. Why?"

"I discovered; I like kids."

She stood to go.

He wanted to hold her, to say it would be all right, but he lacked the words. She leaned forward and kissed him on the cheek.

"Thank you," she said, before crying.

Ben and Hunter watched the crime scene and park people remove Walt's body. Hunter would have liked to explore the second hidey-hole, but his sense that evil was present was too strong. Eventually, Hunter and Ben said their goodbyes and rode southwest out of the canyon and away from the ghosts.

Deputy Blake Young locked his pistol in a gun safe before taking the prisoners their lunch. Blake could have used help, but he and Sheriff Davenport were alone in the courthouse. The five other on-duty officers were patrolling the main highways. Deputy Nalje had the day off. Blake carried four stacked trays into the jail cells. One was for him. Today's menu included chicken pot pie and a brownie.

Tom Kescoli was sleeping it off in the first cell. A deputy found him passed out on the road to Lyman. Tom had spent many nights in lock up. As his name suggested, he had a foot deformity that made him limp. Had the medical people seen Tom early enough in his infancy, they could have corrected his foot. In the old days, the tribe would have left Tom in the bush to die. Instead, Tom's mother had their medicine man sing over the baby. Unfortunately, some problems defy traditional medicine. Tom chose drink as the solution to his physical problems.

"Wake up Tom, it's time for lunch," said Young.

"Go away."

"Tom, you need to eat. I'll leave your lunch here; your cell is open when you want it." Deputy Young put the lunch by the open cell door.

Ralph Langwell took his tray through the bars in the third cell. Ralph was due to be arraigned in court later in the morning. He had a court appointed a lawyer whom he had yet to see. Blake Young left his lunch on a desk across from Tom and Ralph and took the fourth lunch tray to Mel. The jail cells formed an *L* shape, with two cells in one row, and two more around the corner. The sheriff reserved the last cell for the worst criminals. Concrete on both sides isolated the cell from the others.

Young found Mel withered on the floor clutching his stomach. He had one leg twisted under the other.

"What's wrong, Mel?" shouted Deputy Young. "Are you sick?"

Normally, a deputy would not enter a cell alone. Blake should have called for the sheriff, but he knew how much Davenport disliked being disturbed during his afternoon nap. Young set the tray down and pulled out his can of Mace. He had a Taser on his belt, but he didn't imagine he needed anything more than Mace.

"Mel, do you need a doctor?"

Young entered the cell with the Mace pointed toward Mel.

Mel lay motionless on the cell floor. There appeared to be vomit by his face. Blake used his free hand to turn Mel over. He didn't see the sharpened spoon end Mel thrust into his throat. He thumbed the Mace, but the gas sprayed in the wrong direction.

Deputy Young was already bleeding out when Mel took the Taser and keys. Ralph hesitated before he accepted Mel's invitation to join him. He didn't see the Taser or feel Mel break his neck. Mel ran by Tom Kescoli who sat by his cell door. Mel stopped long enough to say, "Yá'át'ééh." Tom left his pot pie and walked back to the far cell. The sight of Ralph Langwell and Deputy Young's dead bodies and the strong smell of blood sent Tom fleeing from the evil that hovered in the cells.

Tom found no one in the main office and no one in the courthouse office. He found Sheriff Davenport asleep on a couch. Fortunately, Tom found Davenport before Mel did.

Davenport ran to check on Langwell and Young. He found the gun safe open and Blake's weapon missing. Tom said he wouldn't go back into the cell area. Davenport checked on the vehicles in front. Young's police cruiser was gone from its space.

Davenport got on the radio and called in all deputies. Some he assigned to set up road blocks, being careful to explain about Blake and the vehicle. Davenport hated losing an officer, especially a relative and such a nice boy as Blake Young. He also realized a prisoner escape would hurt his reelection. He had been planning on running for a state office based on his department ending the killing spree of what the local newspaper called the "Fremont Killers."

In that moment of reflection, he wondered what Mel would do when he discovered that Walt was dead. Once the roadblocks were set up, and a countywide search was begun, he called Deputy Nalje. He'd be needed in the hunt.

~*~

Mai Yázhí was asleep on a couch in the front room of her sister's house when the doorbell rang. Mai checked Ahote sleeping in his crib before going to the door. As a precaution, she picked up her service pistol. She checked the load and pushed off the safety.

Hosteen Nalje smiled into the peephole. Mai opened the door. Ranger Custer Tsinnie stood quietly behind Hunter.

"How nice of you two to visit."

"Are you okay?" Hunter asked.

"Of course, I'm just tired, I…"

"Mel has escaped. He killed Deputy Blake and a prisoner in Loa."

"We don't think you should be here," said Tsinnie.

"He's not going to come here. He's somewhere in the back country or in the canyons. He's not going to drive to Moab. Besides, how would he find me? This isn't my house. It's my sister's house. I'm perfectly fine, and I have this. She showed them the pistol she was holding behind her back."

"And, I have this," said Hunter showing his own automatic. "But, still he got the better of us, and that was before he knew we killed his brother."

"We want to move you," said Tsinnie. "I have friends on the reservation. You will be safe among our people. The whites can't protect you from Mel. He is like a skin-walker."

"I have a job and Ahote. Besides, I can't leave my sister or my mother here if there is any danger."

"You will all go. It is only for a few days. He's driving a sheriff's patrol car. They will catch him soon," said Hunter.

"There's no need to leave. I can arrange something with the local police; a car to watch the house."

"Mai, you aren't listening," said Hunter. "Tsinnie isn't a man who worries. I have never seen him afraid, and yet, he called me. He has been guarding your house for the last two hours waiting for me."

"Little sister," said Tsinnie. "If Mel believes he is a Native American, he will want to avenge his kinsman. He should spend two nights performing the war dance, and a day of feasting. Then he would lead a war party to take women and children captive and kill enemy warriors."

"He's not Diné, and he doesn't have a tribe behind him."

"Yes, but Walt and Mel had help; Fred Gerber, Gladys, and Ralph Langwell, not to mention that woman at the museum, the director. Mel is like the Apache. Dangerous, even as a friend."

"Where can we go?"

"I have friends among the Navajo Cops. You met Sam and Ben. They have a family who will take you in and keep you safe. There is a sheep ranch deep in the heart of Navajo Mountain, on the reservation. They aren't on any map. No one, except the four of us, will know where you are."

"Let me talk to my mother. We'd have to wait until my sister gets home from work."

"Where does she work?" Hunter asked.

"At the visitors center. She works at the information desk."

"I'll get her," said Tsinnie, "after I talk to your mother. We need to leave as soon as possible."

Tsinnie spent several minutes alone with Mai's mother, Janet in the kitchen. When they came out, Janet asked Mai to pack supplies for the baby and for herself. Janet said she would pack for her and Irene.

"Tsinnie, you go ahead and get Irene," said Janet in Diné, "I want to leave in ten minutes. Until then, Gray Wolf will protect us."

"Hunter, will you watch Ahote, while I get a travel bag put together?" asked Mai. In that moment she sounded like the special agent in charge. Mai kissed Hunter on the cheek before running into the back bedroom.

Hunter, Mai, Janet, and Ahote met Tsinnie and Irene at the Visitors Center. Janet insisted that she and Irene ride with Tsinnie and Mai and the baby going with Hunter. The drive took them into Arizona on Highway 191. Then they went west on Highway 160 until they reached Shonto, Arizona.

In Shonto they stopped at the trading post to look at jewelry and buy a gift for their hosts. Mai bought her mother a blue Navajo skirt worn by traditional women. She bought a white headscarf for her sister and herself. Hunter had to laugh at Mai acting like a tourist, yet when she tied the scarf around her hair, he admired her native beauty.

While they were still shopping. Tsinnie made them, hurry and leave. Hunter asked him what was wrong? Tsinnie, said, "That clerk was watching us. The longer we are here, the more he will remember us. Three women and a baby. Remember, Gray Wolf, we are the ones being hunted. We must keep on the move."

Hunter wanted to say, "Don't worry," but Tsinnie was right. Tsinnie's smile was gone. He watched more. He was still calm, but he wasn't as confident.

From Shonto, they followed the road to the Inscription Trading Post on Highway 19. The post had once sold horse blankets. Now it was closed. Instead, they went across the street to a market where Hunter bought sodas. Finally, they were on the road back to Navajo Mountain. Tsinnie used a hand-drawn map to find a dirt road that led to a second dirt road that ended at a trailer and a fence with a sign that said Begay Ranch. They had found the sheep ranch of Sam's brother's oldest daughter Lily, and her husband, Dan Chee.

The ranch was a fenced-in yard with a trailer in the front and a hogan at the back of the property. Dan Chee and his wife, Lily Begay, had two teenaged sons and a three-year-old daughter. They had three dogs and a hundred-plus sheep. Lily Begay was a weaver. She had a traditional flat loom. She learned to weave from her mother and maternal grandmother. The closest trading post was Red Mesa. Lily's grandmother Ann Nez learned to weave with red yarn creating the diamond shaped patterns that the trading post owner wanted.

Lily waited for them at the trailer door. Her two older boys were playing fetch with three dogs. Lily was holding her daughter on her hip. Tsinnie introduced Janet and her daughters, along with little Ahote. When he introduced Hunter, he said his family name and his clans, but then he added, "The White's call him Hunter, but I call him Gray Wolf."

Inside Sam Lapahie and his nephew-in-law, Dan Chee, were playing cards, Gin Rummy. Sam was out of uniform, dressed in jeans and a cowboy shirt.

"Sam, we really appreciate this," said Hunter.

"Hunter, this is my nephew-in-law, Dan Chee. This is his ranch."

Hunter introduced himself and his clans adding, "People call me Hunter."

"Lily's mother was Bitter Water Clan, and my mother was Tangle People. We are related. You are welcome, cousin," said Dan.

"I grew up on a farm like this. Do you have a hogan?"

"At the back of the property. My grandfather built it."

"Have you used it as a sweat lodge?"

"There is a sweat house the men use that is near here. Do you need a ceremony?"

"We need a medicine man who will help us to rid the evil from us. A ceremony for both men and women."

"It sounds like you need an Enemy Way Ceremony."

"Yes, perhaps an Evil Way, as well. We spent too much time among the ghosts."

"I should be able to arrange a ceremony."

~*~

Mel used Deputy Young's car key fob to find the deputy's car. He was hoping for a civilian car. Instead, the headlights blinked, and the horn sounded on a four-year-old Ford explorer with Sheriff painted on the side in green letters.

Mel backed out of the parking space in front of the courthouse. Mel could go west toward Burnsville or turn east toward Hanksville and Moab. Either way, he had at least twenty miles of highway with no alternatives, no alternate routes. West, he would leave Wayne county behind. The problem was there wasn't a decent-sized town to boost a car. What he needed was a grocery store. Down the street were a Dollar store and Royal's food market.

He drove into the Royal's parking lot and parked behind the store. Before leaving the squad car he searched the glove compartment and trunk. In the glove compartment, he found a multi-function pocket knife. In the trunk, he found a riot gun and a bullet-proof vest. He would return for these.

He walked into Royals and bought a coke and a candy bar. Looking at a magazine, he watched a woman with two kids exit a relatively new Toyota. Once she and the kids were moving down a back aisle. Mel ran to her car and used the pocket knife to break the ignition and start the car. Years of boosting cars as a teenager had finally paid off.

He drove slowly out of the Royal's lot. He turned east toward Hanksville. Escape to Las Vegas would have to wait. He planned to visit Agent Yázhí and her family after he killed Deputy Nalje and Ranger Tsinnie.

In Bicknell, Utah he passed by a sheriff cruiser with its flashers going. At the Aquarius Inn, Mel pulled into the parking lot and parked in the space in front of a corner unit. A housekeeping cart sat outside the unit. There were two cars parked in motel spaces.

Mel picked up a bar of soap and a towel from the cart. He washed his face and upper body in a restroom next to the swimming pool. He returned to the Toyota, and feeling better, he sat back and slept.

A man driving a Lexus SUV pulled in just after three in the afternoon. The man looked to be in his thirties. He carried his luggage into unit seven on the ground floor. Mel figured he had ten to twenty minutes to wait. The man would either stay in or leave to find food and drink. Either way, there were opportunities. Mel needed money and a change of clothes.

Deputy Young's wallet provided fifty-seven dollars, and four credit cards. Enough for food and gas, but nothing else. Cash was the thing. When the man didn't come back out, Mel decided he'd have to go in. Mel did not think of himself as naturally violent, but sometimes the situation required a measure of violence and insanity.

Mel spent two summers working for a traveling carnival during high school. The first year he was a ticket taker on a ride, the Whip. The second year he was a shill, or the pitchman for a ring toss booth. In the game, you had to toss a ring over a milk bottle to win a prize, a stuffed elephant, or a teddy bear. The game wasn't rigged like some. It was simply that the rings had so little clearance, they could only go over a bottle if they were dropped directly down on the bottle. Mel's job was to wait until there was a large crowd, and then using a very practiced throw, he'd drop a winner and walk away with a bear. In playing his role, Mel had to change clothes and even wear a beard. Over time, he learned Three-card Monte and the Pigeon Drop in addition to many small cons the carnies played in the booths.

In the carnival, Mel also learned about bigotry and the value of friends. One time in Heber, Utah a pair of cowboys recognized Mel from the night before. They grabbed Mel and threatened to call the police. Immediately a call, "Hey Rube," ran through the midway and a dozen barkers and shills were there to separate the cowboys from Mel. No one was hurt; Mel learned the value of family and the cowboys got a teddy bear. After that, Mel started carrying a knife, and later an automatic.

Now, he picked up the deputy's Glock, and put it under the towel he'd stolen from the maid's cart. Certain that no one was watching, Mel got out of the Toyota and walked from the corner of the building to unit seven and knocked on the door.

"Yes."

"Maintenance, Sir. I'm supposed to check the air conditioning."

"Can you come back?"

"It will only take a few minutes." Mel was about to leave when the door opened. The man was wearing a robe. He had been in the shower.

"Just a few minutes, and I'll be gone," said Mel, stepping into the motel room. Mel showed the gun and told the man to sit on the bed. Ten minutes later, Mel left the motel room dressed in blue dress slacks, a white cotton dress shirt, and carrying a suitcase. He deposited the bags in the SUV. Before driving out, Mel transferred the shotgun and vest from the Toyota. With luck, it would be a day before the maids found the body of Ronny Davis bound and gagged in his motel room.

Driving east, Mel practiced saying he was Ronny Davis; from Salt Lake City, born on July 24, 1990. He didn't look very much like Davis but shaved and wearing a BYU ball cap, he might make it through a road block.

In Hanksville, Mel bought a soda, and a Chick-O-Stick candy bar. When Mel asked for a phone book, the attendant asked, "Who are you looking for? You get to know everyone in a town this size," said the counterman.

"Hosteen Nalje," said Mel. "We were in the service together."

"Hosteen, oh, you mean Hunter."

"That's right, Hunter."

"He lives at West 100 South, but I think he's gone."

"That's a shame. I might as well check. Which way is 100 South?"

The attendant looked at Mel oddly. All the towns in Utah were laid out in a grid. "His trailer is three blocks that way." He pointed south.

Mel drove by the trailer three times before parking across the street. Eventually, a man came out of the trailer next door. He had his right hand in his pants pocket.

"Need something?" he asked.

"No. I am waiting for Hunter. He said he'd be home. We were in the service together."

"Hunter had to leave. Not sure when he's coming back. He's in Moab. I am taking care of his horse. What's your name?"

"Davis. Ronny Davis. I'm staying at the Aquarius Inn in Bicknell. But only for a day. When Hunter comes back, will you tell him I called? Remember, Ronny Davis."

"Sure."

"Thanks."

Mel left as quickly as he could without fleeing.

It was over an hour before Kim Wheatley called the sheriff's office in Loa to mention Ronny Davis's visit. By then Mel was in Green River where he rented a room at the Sleepy Hollow Motel and ate pizza at the Chow Hound across the street. So far, his luck had held. Mel knew that the local police could not set up a road block on a federal highway. If he didn't have business in Moab, he could be safely in Denver in two days of driving. The problem was blood had to be avenged. Hunter Nalje and his ranger friends had taken Mel's half-brother and his lover from him in the same week. Blood demanded blood.

Hunter and Tsinnie sat on log stumps behind Dan Chee's trailer listening to the sheep and watching the sun set. It had reached 100 degrees, and it would be hours before the air cooled. Hunter was drinking iced tea, and Tsinnie drinking water. Each man had a gun on the ground beside his stump. The women were in the hogan weaving and talking about babies and men. Sam had gone into work, and Dan and the two older boys were out on the ATV rounding up sheep. Across the scrub flatland, Navajo Mountain was visible. The darkening sky had streaks of red and blue.

Mai came out of the hogan wiping her face with a towel. Tsinnie stood up and offered her his seat, which she accepted. He wandered toward the hogan.

Hunter and Mai had spoken little in the car and this was one of the first times they were alone. Hunter knew it was too soon to talk about Mel and what happened if that time ever came. However, the cop in him didn't know what else to talk about, so his silence matched Mai's.

Looking toward the dark blue mountains, Mai sighed.

"This is how it was two hundred years ago when we owned the land," said Hunter.

"It is very beautiful," said Mai.

"So are you," said Hunter, immediately regretting his words.

"I wish you wouldn't. I still feel like I am covered in filth. The department wants me to see a therapist. It's required before I can return to duty."

"Having someone to talk to could help," said Hunter.

"What I need is a cleansing. I need a medicine man to help me cleanse my soul." Mai started to cry.

"I asked Dan about having a ceremony here. He said he would work on arranging one."

"It needs to be soon. I feel like there is a hole in my soul, and all the good in me, my life spirit, is leaving my body."

Hunter looked at Mai in the firelight. The bruises on her face were only the most obvious signs of the damage Walt had done to her as a woman, as a human being.

"There must be something I can do. Something for you; something for Ahote."

"Ahote needs a Ma'iitsoh, a protector—guardian. You can be his Gray Wolf. He needs more than I can give right now."

"That isn't true. I watched you with him today. What happened to you didn't make you any less a mother. The rest will come in time."

"I hope so," she said crying, again. "I tried so hard."

Saying nothing more, Mai ran back to the hogan. Moments later Tsinnie came out and rejoined Hunter on the logs.

"Mai was crying," said the older ranger.

"She said needs a ceremony," said Hunter.

214

"She told her sister you promised to take care of Ahote, and then they all started crying. Women have secrets in their hearts that we men never share, we never learn. Secrets we can never understand."

The men sat for a time without speaking. Finally, Hunter said, "In all this time together, you never told me why your parents named you Custer."

"My father and Uncle James were watching an old Errol Flynn movie on the night I was born. Flynn was playing George Custer. Naturally, they were rooting for Sitting Bull. Dad wanted to call me Errol and Uncle James suggested calling me George. I guess they both said Custer at the same time and laughed. From that moment on I was Custer on legal documents. I became Tsinnie, the Bony One, when I was older."

"Tsinnie also means Old Tree. You are like the great trees, steady and solid. You give shelter and shade."

"Nephew, you should have been a poet. You have a poet's way of speaking."

"I only tell the truth."

"What was that?" Tsinnie reached down for his rifle. "It looked like a coyote."

Hunter fell to the ground. He heard a bullet whiz by before he heard the gun's report. The bullet missed Hunter's head and exploded instead in the trailer's aluminum siding. Tsinnie grabbed his rifle and crawled toward the hogan. The hogan door opened, and the light from the room shown on Tsinnie.

"Get down and turn your lights off," Tsinnie shouted, as he crawled out of the light. Another bullet impacted just in front of Tsinnie's face. He rolled into the shadow of the hogan. More shots rang out.

"Mai, call for help," shouted Hunter. He crouched behind the stump. Counting to five, he stayed low as he ran half way across the backyard. Hunter wanted to hop the fence and run to the shooter—to Mel.

That's what he wants, thought Hunter. He has moved already. He will circle and attack the trailer or the hogan from the side.

"Gray Wolf," Tsinnie called in Diné. "Stay where you are. You must protect the women. I'll look around."

"Tsinnie, we should wait for backup."

Hunter strained to see beyond the fence in the dark. The fence line was visible, and the shape of the mountain behind. Something moved at the fence. A rifle shot broke the silence. Then a second, and a third shot rang out. A man lay on the ground beside the fence. Hunter couldn't tell if it was Tsinnie or Mel.

A police car siren called out in the distance. In his experience, this was the time with the most danger. The attacker had little time, and the defenders were likely to let their guard drop. Even when the tribal police arrived, they wouldn't be safe from a sniper. Hunter raised his rifle into a shooting position and sighted on the fence line. The man was gone. Nothing moved.

A police car, with lights and siren blaring, pulled into the yard in front of the trailer. Sam and Ben bailed out of the car with guns drawn. A second car was close behind. Hunter dropped to the ground and called out.

"We are in the back. We have a sniper. Be careful."

"Is that you Hunter?" called Sam.

"Yes."

"Where is the shooter?"

"He was outside the fence to the west, but he could be anywhere now. He might be wearing a coyote skin."

"Where are the women?"

"They are safe."

"Can they move?"

"No."

"I understand."

One of the patrol cars came around the trailer, with the headlights pointed toward the fence. An officer stood behind the open driver's door and used a spotlight to search the fence line. Just to the left of the hogan, Tsinnie lay on the ground.

"Officer down," screamed Hunter. He ran across the yard to Tsinnie. The officer using the spotlight turned the light beam away and searched the desert beyond. A second officer called for medical assistance.

"Tsinnie," said Hunter as he searched the fallen ranger. Blood covered his stomach and leg. "Where are you hit?"

"In the stomach. I may not see the morning."

"Don't talk like that, help is on the way. Let's get some pressure on the wound."

"I'm thirsty."

Hunter took off his shirt and applied it to the front of the wound. "I need a pressure bandage," he called. "I need help."

The officer by the passenger door, ran from the car carrying a medical pack. As he passed the side of the hogan, another shot rang out, and he dropped out of sight. The officer at the car door fired a semi-automatic AK-15. He was spraying bullets back and forth across the back of the fence. Hunter crawled to the fallen policeman. He was uninjured. Hunter grabbed a pressure bandage and crawled back to Tsinnie. "Nephew," whispered Tsinnie. "I like Mai's mother. It would have been nice to be your father-in-law."

"You will be, Uncle. Stay with me."

"I'm not sure I can. Remember me."

Tsinnie closed his eyes. Hunter picked up the Marlin rifle beside Tsinnie. It was the lever action Marlin his neighbor Kim had loaned him.

"Hunter, it's Sam. Don't answer, just listen. Medical is on the way, and I have called in a helicopter and more officers. We will get you out of here. Ben is coming to you. Stay put."

Good to his word, Ben came around the hogan on his stomach. Hunter crawled to him when he reached the fence.

"One of the policemen is on the ground playing dead," said Hunter. "Tsinnie is shot. I'm not sure if he is alive. He's bleeding out."

"You and I are going to drag him to the front," said Ben. "There should be an EMT here by then. Are you ready?"

"Yes. Whatever happens, don't stop. Dead or alive, we are moving him to the front. No one gets left behind," said Hunter.

"Okay, let's go," said Ben.

They ran to the fence, and each man grabbed one side of Tsinnie's vest. Without stopping, they dragged the ranger to the front of the trailer. Another police car and an EMT van pulled into the yard. Two medics jumped out and transferred Tsinnie from Hunter and Ben without saying half a dozen words. They worked on the ranger, even as Hunter and Ben joined the other officers in the front of the trailer.

"Will he make it?" asked Ben.

"I don't think so," said Hunter. "The women and children are in the hogan. We need to get them to safety."

"They are safe, right there. We need to find your shooter."

"It's Mel."

"That doesn't seem possible. How could Mel elude a four-state police dragnet and find you?"

"He's a yee nahgloshii, a skin-walker."

"You don't believe that, and neither do I. Let's go help, Sam."

They followed behind a second squad car as it drove around the trailer and parked next to the hogan door.

A police helicopter came into view, its searchlight moving back and forth across the land beyond the fence. The helicopter searched for an hour without finding signs of the shooter.

While the copter searched from the air, three police cars searched on the ground. In the relative safety created by the presence of so many police, the women and children were moved into the trailer.

219

Dan and the boys had been stopped on their way home. Eventually, they were allowed back, too.

For a time, the group ate and drank without talking. Finally, Sam took the floor. As always, he spoke in a low, calm voice.

"I brought Janet and her family here because they were in danger and they are friends; they are family. I thought they would be safe here. I underestimated this Anglo's ability. Perhaps as he claims, he shares our ancestry. Hunter believes he is a skin-walker, a witch. The fact that he is evil does not mean he has magical powers. Yet somehow, he found a sheep ranch that isn't on the maps. It may not matter how he found us. In the morning, we must move again. However, the cop in me is convinced it wasn't magic or evil spirits that Mel used to find us. So, I have a simple question, did any of you talk to anyone about where you were going or about visitors staying on the ranch. If you did, please raise your hand."

At first, no one raised his or her hand. Then Hunter raised his hand. Soon, all the hands except the two babies were raised.

"Let's start with you Hunter. Who did you tell?" Sam asked.

"I told my neighbor I was going to Moab for several days. He is taking care of my horse."

"No one else?"

"No."

"Mai?"

"I called my boss in Salt Lake, and the head ranger in Moab."

"Janet."

"I called Irene at the ranger station. To tell her Tsinnie was coming."

"Irene."

"I told my boss, and another girl at the desk, I had to go help a family member in the Nation."

"Dan."

"At the feed store, I mentioned we had relatives visiting."

Each person, except Lily, had told someone, including Sam and Ben.

"All little crumbs of bread, but enough for a good cop. We knew Mel was dangerous, and a good rifle shot. Now we know he is a bloodhound. We cannot be so careless, again."

Sam took a moment to look at each person.

"Or, maybe we need to leave a false trail of bread. One that leads to a bullet, or death row," said Hunter.

They talked until first light. Dan Chee, Hunter, and Ben went to the back fences with their hunting rifles and binoculars. They saw nothing. With two other officers, they walked from the perimeter, back for a half a mile. Hunter found coyote signs, and several spent bullet casings. They also found moccasin tracks mixed with the coyote prints. The shooter had to walk into the area, but where the shooter entered the area wasn't obvious. They saw no vehicle signs for over a mile back.

Sam was waiting for them at the fence.

"Tsinnie had been taken to the Kayenta Health Center in Kayenta, Arizona," Sam said. "His condition is listed as 'grave.'"

The Health Center was one of only two hospitals within ninety miles of the ranch. The other hospital was in Page. Both facilities were designed with Navajo traditions and beliefs in mind. The emergency room, where Tsinnie was admitted faced the morning sun, where life started. The facility had a room for medicine men and a hogan for families.

"I am staying here," said Dan Chee. He had been quiet most of the night, smoking cigarettes and drinking coffee. "I have to protect the ranch and the sheep. Lily and the kids can stay with her mother. There is no reason for this mad man to bother them."

"I hope that is right. Your dad will not forgive me if the sheep are harmed," said Sam.

"My two younger brothers can work the ranch with me for a while. They are good with a rifle." Dan gave a grim smile.

"Now we need to find a place for Mai and her family," said Sam.

"I have friends in Shiprock. I could stay with them," said Irene.

"How about going back to Moab?" asked Mai. "If he is here in the Nation, he's not going back to Moab. The chances of being picked up in a road block are too great." For the first time, Mai sounded like a cop.

"By that reasoning, you should come stay with me in Hanksville. Or stay in Loa," said Hunter.

"He will assume we will go back to work eventually," said Mai.

"I'd like to be with Tsinnie," said Janet. "Having someone holding your hand can make all the difference after surgery."

"Honestly, I'd like to be there too," said Mai.

"Okay, here's the plan," said Sam. "Dan, call your brothers and get them here A-S-A-P. I'll arrange for an officer to stay with you, at least for a day. Irene, call your friends in Shiprock. We will have a car take you there. Janet, I'll take you to Tsinnie. Ben, you will go with Mai, Ahote, and Hunter to Hanksville."

"Why not go to one safe location?" asked Hunter.

"No place is safe from a skin-walker, Nephew. However, if he is watching us and we leave and all go to Kayenta and then divide into four cars and go in four different directions, what is he going to do?"

"Follow the one he hates most, or the car with the most people," said Hunter.

"*Follow* is the key word," said Sam. "What if we set up roadblocks outside of Kayenta? There's one road to Shiprock and Hanksville. We are certain to pick him up. The hospital might be harder to protect."

"I'm going to stay with Tsinnie. I want to make sure he will make it before I leave for Hanksville," said Hunter.

"I feel the same," said Mai.

"Okay, we'll all go to the hospital, and then we'll individually sneak out, except for Hunter. He becomes the bait."

"Hunter and I," said Mai. "We started this. Plus, Mel and I have unfinished business."

"What about Ahote?" Janet asked.

"He can go with Irene or you, Mom. He spends more time with you, and he will be safe. I have to do this."

They made a show of moving out of the trailer and leaving in a convoy of police cars. Even Dan Chee left. He would come back under cover of night with his brothers, and a police officer as protection. The plan was moving, and so was Mel.

~*~

Mel watched the cars leave until he was certain which car had Hunter and Mai. He didn't expect them to be together, but they were making it easy. His car was hidden a half mile off the dirt road behind the ranch. He considered killing all the rancher's sheep, but he didn't have the time. He jogged back to his car. Mel recognized the foolishness of his feud with Hunter and Tsinnie, but he was alone in the world now, so it didn't matter.

Mel missed getting them in Moab. He was still in Green River when they left. Dressed in nice pants, a blue Polo shirt, and a sports coat, Mel visited the visitors center looking for Mai. There he learned Mai and her sister Irene were on vacation. He called the information desk from a phone in the lobby and asked for Irene. Again, he was told she was on vacation. When he explained that he had important time-sensitive documents for Irene, the receptionist said, "Irene mentioned going to a ranch in the Navajo Nation."

In jail, Deputy Blake told Mel that a pair of tribal cops had taken his brother, Walt out. Sam Lapahie and Ben-something. It took a while before Mel tracked down Sam Lapahie. He called several stations along the border of Utah until he found a Sergeant Sam Lapahie, working out of Kayenta, Arizona. After that, it was a simple matter of following Lapahie until he drove to a sheep ranch outside of Navajo Mountain.

Once Mel was certain where Hunter and Mai were hiding, he found an isolated gun store primed for robbery. He had to kill the boy behind the counter, but he took a treasure trove of weapons, ammo, and more cash. He even found an outfitter store that was selling coyote pelts. Mel had to smile at the thought of all the superstitious Navajo men seeing a man wearing a coyote fur as a hat or coat. Mel was certain that seeing a man in a coyote skin would mess with their heads, as much as a 30-30 through the brain. In his plan, Hunter and Tsinnie would receive both.

Like all good plans, a breeze, a change in the light, and the target moving at the wrong moment ruined a perfect shot, and now, Mel had to improvise.

Hunter sat in a chair at the end of the bed trying to read the Navajo Times, the Diné bi Naltsoos. A local inn had burned down overnight, and a veteran steer-wrestler had grappled his way to the top. The story on the second page described a shootout with police and a suspect on a sheep ranch in Navajo Mountain the day before. The article said a National Park Service Ranger, Custer Tsinnie was in critical condition at Kayenta Regional.

Hunter brushed back tears. Tsinnie had been in and out of consciousness over the last four hours. In twenty-four hours, his condition changed from grave to guarded. Hunter had decided to stay with Tsinnie another day. Mai was at a nearby motel guarded by two officers. She sent her mother, sister, and son to Shiprock with two officers in an unmarked car. Hunter and Mai had discussed their options. It was a risk sending her mother and son away, but if they slipped away unseen, they would soon be impossible to find. The plan was to make Hunter and Tsinnie the easiest targets. At the end of the bed, under the sports section of the Navajo Times, Hunter had a new Glock 18.

"Hunter, is that you?" Tsinnie's voice sounded weak and dry. "Is there water?"

Hunter fed Tsinnie water from a plastic glass with a straw.

"I did not expect to see you in the next world," said Tsinnie.

"We are still in the world of the people. You are hard to kill."

"Did you get him?"

"He is still on the loose. I've baited a hook."

"What is the bait?"

Hunter patted the older man's leg and lifted the sports section to reveal his automatic. "You were available, and you didn't complain."

"Do I get hazard pay?"

"That will depend on Mel."

"So, how am I doing, because I feel like a gopher who has been chased by a coyote?"

"It's afternoon. Your surgery, yesterday, lasted four hours. The doctors called your condition guarded, but improved, which means you might still be my father-in-law."

"I would be honored, but now I could sleep." Tsinnie closed his eyes. Hunter turned back to the paper. He and Mai planned to have dinner together at the hotel at six that evening.

A nurse stuck her head in the doorway. "Are you Deputy Nalje?"

"Yes, what is it?"

"You have a call."

"A call? Do you know who it is?"

"A Sheriff Davenport."

"Can I take the call in here?"

"No, there is a phone by the nurse's station at the end of the hall."

"Can you stay with my friend?"

"I have other patients. Do you want me to tell the sheriff you will call him back?"

"Just stay here a minute, and I'll be back."

"Oh, all right." The nurse stepped in, and Hunter ran down the hall to the nurse's station. The nurse at the desk had a chart in her hand. She was Navajo and very pretty.

"Yá'át'ééh. I am Deputy Sheriff Nalje. I am Bit'ahnii born for Táchii'nii. My cheii is Tódích'íi'nii, and my nálí is Ta'neeszahnii. The nurse said there was a call for me."

"Is this how you pick up women?"

"What?"

"You introduce yourself formally and say you have a phone call."

She laughed, and Hunter laughed, too.

"I might try it in the future if you think it would work."

"It might. My name is Sharon Begay."

"So, what about my call, Sharon?"

"Really, there isn't a call."

"Why would the nurse tell me?"

He ran back to Tsinnie's hospital room. He didn't hear Sharon ask, "What nurse?" The hospital room door was open, and no nurse. Tsinnie was sleeping. His eyes were closed. He had a slight smile on his face. On his lap was an obsidian stone-age knife the nurse used to slit his throat. A massive amount of blood from his severed carotid artery covered his chest.

Hunter called to Sharon, "I need help, and call security," he yelled. On the pillow, a folded note lay by Tsinnie's head.

Hastíín Nalzheehíí,

Now, it is just you and me. I have your girlfriend. We need to finish this. I'll meet you at the Great Gallery Wall in Horseshoe Canyon at dawn (6:00 a.m.) in two days. If you want to see the girl alive, come alone. Otherwise, she will die in a hole.

Maíí' (Coyote).

~*~

Hunter described the nurse to the security officer knowing it was useless. He called Mai's cellphone. A man answered.

"Who is this," Hunter asked.

"I am a police officer. Who is this?"

"Where is Mai Yázhí."

"Tell me who you are first."

"Deputy Sheriff Hosteen Nalje, Wayne County. I am working with Agent Yázhí. What has happened?"

"There were shots fired in the parking lot. We called for backup, and I went to see what was happening. My partner stayed outside the door guarding the agent. When I left, she was standing just inside the room watching, too. I guess she came out of the room."

"Is your partner dead?"

"No, they used Tasers."

"They?"

"He thinks there were two men or two people. I called for road blocks and an APB, but there are too many dirt roads out of here. Any idea where he might go?"

"Maybe."

"Are you coming here?"

"No."

"How's your friend, the Park Ranger?"

"He didn't make it."

"I'm sorry for that. He had a lot of friends here."

"Yes, it helps to have friends."

Hunter spent a moment, looking at Custer Tsinnie. They'd only known each other for a week. A lifetime in seven days. He felt the way he had when his father died, and his Uncle Joe. He used his cellphone to call Ben Nabahe.

Hunter turned on the headlamp he had attached to his baseball cap. At four thirty, it was cold on the high desert flats. Hunter had on running pants, a long-sleeve shirt, and a dark hoodie. Under his shirt was a level four bulletproof vest he borrowed from Kim Wheatley. Over the hoodie, he had on a hunting vest, filled with ammo, and small items that might prove useful, like matches and a candle. He carried a hydration pack. In a shoulder holster was his Glock, and he had the lever action Marlin with the scope that Kim Wheatley had loaned Tsinnie.

Following the trail down to the canyon floor, he had no idea what would happen, or why Mel wanted to meet like this. Hunter didn't feel prepared. He was alone, without a partner. He remembered Custer Tsinnie and brushed back tears. Another day, Hunter might have wanted revenge. Now, all that mattered was Mai Yázhí.

Hunter used his headlamp for the first mile, and then he walked in the dark using the moonlight and his senses to guide the way. The smaller painted galleries were silent. The ghosts were sleeping. Hunter stopped to get his bearings. The Great Gallery was very near. He pulled out his pistol, pushed off safe, and jacked a shell. Hunter put the Marlin on his left shoulder with his finger on the trigger. He couldn't decide whether to go to the wall and wait or move into the cottonwoods and wait for better light. Hunter inched his way to the cliff face. He followed the curve of the cliff until he reached the main wall of paintings. Birds were moving about in the cottonwoods.

He rounded the bend leading to the Great Gallery. The paintings danced above the river bed. Hunter could stay with the wall or move down and crawl along the dry creek. At the end of the two-hundred-foot-long wall, he saw the Holy Ghost.

Below the paintings was a narrow path with large broken boulders from the wall. The dry river bed was another thirty feet below. This is where most visitors stand to take pictures and admire the primitive art.

Hunter stopped, put his right hand against the wall, and let his eyes adjust to the blue-black sky. In the darkness, he might be mistaken for one of the smaller figures. In less than an hour, he would be a visible target. He had no way of finding Mai, so he waited.

He had heard Mel and Mai before he saw them. Mel yelled at her to mind her step. He sounded angry. They came into view. Mai had a black hood over her head and a rope around her neck. Mel had dressed her in clothes like those worn by the Fremont Culture People—a white dress. He held a gun against her head. Mel walked behind Mai. She appeared to be barefoot.

When they reached the river bed below the Holy Ghost, Mel forced her stop and squat on her knees. He knelt behind her keeping the gun on her head. Hunter unslung the Marlin and sited on Mel. He had a possible shot. *Mel must have a backup,* thought Hunter.

"Deputy," Mel called. "It's time to talk."

Hunter knelt and sighted the rifle cross hairs on Mel's head.

"I'm fine where I am," called Hunter.

"Are you alone?"

"There is no one with me. Why are we here?"

"I have artifacts to collect. They will buy me a trip across the border and a new life in Mexico."

"I thought you said you are Native American. The past should remain here. The spirits will not like you exploiting our ancestors."

"What spirits? The paintings on these walls? If I could, I'd cut the ghosts off the wall and sell the panels to the highest bidder. All that matters is getting the money I need and evening the score."

"What score?"

"My brother and Gladys need avenging. Your friend might be payment for Walt, but not Gladys. Blood needs blood."

"Haven't you killed enough people already?"

"I rather like killing people, and I plan to continue. The question is, do I kill you first, or Agent Yázhí? This is where it started. It seemed fitting it ends here."

"What do you expect me to do?"

"I expect you to drop your weapons, and exchange places with Agent Yázhí. If you do that, I will let her go. All I ask is that she stays to watch me kill you, and then she is free to go."

"Even if I wanted to make the exchange, why should I believe you wouldn't kill her, too. This makes little sense."

"Of course, it does. Honor among thieves. You stole Gladys from me. So, I am stealing you from your Bright Flower."

"You will never get out of this canyon."

"Who will stop me, the ghosts? I came prepared. I have two horses back in the cottonwoods." He laughed, the sound echoing in on the canyon walls.

"I have been one step ahead of you most of the time," shouted Mel. "All the people you talked to were my friends; people I worked with, or who worked for me. Gladys called me the moment you left, and a friend at the museum called to warn me you were coming to the reservoir. Even the information lady at the visitor's center in Moab was happy to tell me where Mai's sister was going. I have a way with women. After last night, even Agent Yázhí is coming over to my side. That's why I know she will want to watch me slit your throat. You fucked up, Man Hunter. Put down your rifle and pistol and come here."

"Send Agent Yázhí half way, and I'll leave my rifle here and come half way to you. That way we both have pistols."

"Like in the Old West. The sheriff meeting the bad guy for a gunfight in the street. The setting isn't quite right, but we have an audience, even if they are silent." Mel gestured to the ghosts.

Hunter set the Marlin on the ground and put his pistol in his pants pocket. Mel yelled at Mai to get up and pushed her toward Hunter. He walked behind Mai keeping her between himself and Hunter. After several steps, he stuck his pistol in his waistband and used both hands to push her to the middle of the Great Gallery where she stopped.

Hunter advanced half the distance and stopped, too.

"Mai, Aạ'?" He called, asking if she was well.

Mai said nothing back. *She must be gagged*, he thought.

"Mai, Ąą' ha'íí baa naniná?" He tried again.

Mai was thirty feet away with Mel behind her. Hunter was in the open.

"Take the hood off. I want to see her. Make sure she is okay."

"You do it. She is almost to you. I've come as far as I am going to," said Mel.

"Mai, ni'níłtłáád, Stop," he called. She kept walking to him. Mai blocked his view and a shot at Mel. She seemed to be almost running. If he stepped aside or tried to push her out of his way, Mel would have an easy shot.

The first rays of sunlight blinked over the opposite side of the canyon wall. Mai turned to look at the sunlight. It was as if she could see out of the mask or sense the light. Hunter jumped sideways to his left. He pulled the pistol out of his pants pocket. Mel was less than thirty feet from Hunter. Mel had his pistol stretched out in his right hand in a shooting position. Hunter heard a shot and fired back. A blossom of red spread across Mel's white shirt. He looked at Hunter and then at the line of ghosts on the wall. High above the ghosts, Ben Nabahe had the rifle on his shoulder.

"We will meet in the next world," Mel managed to say, "and soon." He fell forward and didn't move. Hunter waved at Ben. Ben pumped the rifle twice.

"Mai, it's all over. Mel's dead."

Mai turned and walked toward Hunter. Somehow Mai had gotten her hands free, and they were at her side.

Hunter took a step sideways. Mai shifted her direction.

"Mai, you have to stop where you are." She kept coming.

Hunter put his hands up to stop her.

She lifted her right hand. There was a stone knife with a black blade in her hand. Her attack was practiced and coordinated. She held the knife for a downward slash. Hunter used his left arm to defend against the stone blade, at the same time hitting her in the face with his right fist. She dropped to the sand. Hunter fell back, the blade had cut through his jacket and bitten into his flesh. Hunter pushed the knife aside and pulled the hood off her head. His attacker was Susan Vaughn the director from the museum. Hunter realized; she could have been the nurse in the hospital wearing a wig.

She got up and came at him again, screaming like a mad person. Hunter shot her in the right shoulder. The bullet spun her around. She went down on one knee, shifted the knife to her left hand, and tried to rise. Hunter knocked the knife out of her hand.

"Where is Agent Yázhí?"

"I need medical assistance."

"You are the director of that museum."

"Get me help."

"Where is Agent Yázhí?"

"She's here in the canyon. Just like Mel promised."

"Where is she? Show me, and I'll call for help."

"She's dead. We performed a ritual sacrifice. We cut her throat."

"I don't believe you. The ghosts say she is alive."

"Don't be ridiculous."

"You will bleed out unless I help you. If she's dead, take me to her body, and I'll get you the aid you need."

"She's in a cave in those boulders. Now call for help." She pointed to the boulder with Walt's cave.

"I have to see the body. Come with me."

"I'm not going anywhere. I'm staying here."

She sat down under a cottonwood.

Hunter gave her a compression bandage from a vest pocket. "Push it hard against the bullet hole." He walked to Mel and checked for any sign of life.

Hunter picked up Mel's automatic, put it in his pocket, and put his own gun back in its holster. Certain that Susan would be no threat, he ran to the boulders. He was on the first level of rocks when Susan stood up and ran east toward the park entrance.

Hunter wasn't worried. He doubted she would make the parking lot, and if she did, she'd find a deputy waiting for her. The real problem was if she was lying and Mai was somewhere else; or worse, if Mai was, in fact, dead.

At the top of the boulders, Hunter found the canvas that covered the cave entrance and pulled it back. He shined the light from his headlamp into the hold. Mai was naked and bound, her body curled in a ball. Dried blood covered her stomach and chest. She looked almost peaceful. As if, she had joined the ghosts.

Hunter sat back from the entrance. The presence of death and the sense of evil in the cave overwhelmed him. Mai and Tsinnie had been the only people in years to mean anything in Hunter's life, and now they were dead. The coyote had bested the Gray Wolf.

Hunter moaned and started to chant. He wasn't a singer, but he knew the words. He needed to start the process to drive his enemy from this sacred place. His wailing chant caught on the wind. The ghosts called back to him.

"Hunter. . ."

Hunter stopped chanting and listened to the wind in the cottonwoods.

"Hunter. . ."

Hunter moved back to the cave entrance. Mai had an arm raised in the air. She was alive.

"Hunter is that you?"

"I'll come down to you."

"Hurry, I'm hurt, bad."

Hunter looked for the ladder.

"Mai, where is the ladder. Mai."

She didn't answer.

Hunter called Ben on his cellphone. "Send help, Mai is injured. She's in the cave by the boulders. I'm going to climb down to help her, but I don't think I can climb out with her. I'll need help, and soon. Oh, and watch for a blonde with a gunshot wound in her right shoulder. She's coming out."

Using his hands and feet pressed against the cave walls, Hunter managed to shinny down to the bottom of the cave. Mai was curled up, and her breathing was shallow.

"Mai I'm here." Hunter spread a little water on her lips and then used his wet fingers to wipe some of the dried blood from her face.

"No more. Please, no more. I can't," She pushed his hand away.

"Mai, it's Hunter."

"Hunter. Mel hurt me. I tried," she said. "I tried."

Hunter took her in his arms. He wet her lips again and wiped the blood from her face and forehead. Gently, he kissed her head and lips.

"Ma'iitsoh," she said, "where were you?" She closed her tear-filled eyes.

 Hunter watched Ahote walk across the room to his grandmother. He kept his arms out for balance. Each step a new adventure. Each step strengthening his mastery of his world. He picked up a wooden rattle and shook it. The sound made him laugh. He carried the rattle over to his mother. Mai sat in an overstuffed chair, wrapped in a blanket. Her eyes followed the boy, and she smiled at his antics, yet she didn't take the rattle when offered, and she didn't speak. Ahote took the rattle to Hunter. For a time, Hunter played hide and seek with the rattle and then peekaboo. Hunter picked up Ahote and held him in his arms until Mai's mother, Janet, took the sleeping baby to his room.

Mai had become distant since her rescue in the canyon. She spent hours staring out the window, her eyes unfocused, seeing a different world. Sometimes she'd cry out in her sleep shouting, "No more, I can't."

Hunter had hoped that when Mai was with her family, she would recover. For a time, she seemed to be her old self. She took care of Ahote and talked about returning to work. Then, she grew worse. She seemed to turn in on herself. The Park Service made her see a psychologist. When therapy and drugs didn't work, Janet strung together Ghost Beads for Mai to wear. Janet believed Mel was a skin-walker whose evil remained inside Mai. Janet said Mai needed a healing ceremony. She asked Hunter to arrange for an Enemy Way Ceremony to be performed in the canyon as soon as possible, in the summer.

Janet returned and sat on the arm of Mai's chair. She stroked Mai's long black hair. "She is worse today."

"The psychologist said it could take time," said Hunter.

"Police psychologist. What does she know? That man was a witch. Mai needs a ceremony."

"I have a medicine man scheduled to performed the Enemy Way and Evil Way ceremonies this summer in the canyon. I just hope it isn't too late." Hunter took Mai's hand. She looked at him showing no sign of recognition.

"She is possessed by evil spirits," said Janet.

Hunter took Mai's fingers in his right hand. He had fallen in love with Special Agent Mai Yázhí—a smart, competent policewoman. *This* woman was someone else. She looked at him with little sign that she was alive. Hunter feared that Mai was beyond a medicine man's help. She was lost.

"Perhaps the ghosts will help," said Hunter.

CHAPTER 20 - Wednesday, December 7, 2016

 It is dark at the base of the canyon by the Ghost Wall. A light mist covers the canyon floor. Crows are calling in the distance. The paintings on the wall seem to float in the mist. The painted figures look out in silence. The first rays of sunlight creeps over the ridge of the canyon.

The faces and eyes on the ghosts are gradually illuminated and then their armless and legless bodies. The whole wall seems to come alive with a new day.

About the Author

Roger C. Lubeck is the vice president on the board of directors of the California Writers' Club and Immediate Past President for the Redwood Branch of the California Writers Club for 2017-2020. He was the editor-in-chief on four anthologies, and a memoir by Samuel C. Chandler. Roger's published works include eleven novels, two business books, business articles, two dozen short stories and poems, two produced ten-minute plays, and a 1st place winner in a short story contest. Roger is developing a screenplay for *Ghosts in Horseshoe Canyon*.

Roger lives in California and divides his time between writing, publishing, photography, and business consulting. He was the president of Corporate Behavior Analysts, Ltd., a leadership and management consulting firm. Roger is president and publisher at It Is What It Is Press. He has over thirty years consulting in real estate services, healthcare, higher education, manufacturing, and mental health. Roger is the author of articles on customer service, leadership, management, marketing, and sales. He and Chris Hanson are the authors of two business books written for the title insurance industry. He offers courses on writing and self-publishing.

Roger has a doctorate in Experimental Psychology from Utah State University and earned his master's and bachelor's degrees in Behavioral Psychology from Western Michigan University. In his career, Roger has been a business consultant, workshop leader, retreat facilitator, public speaker, speechwriter, assistant professor, researcher, parent trainer, and dog catcher. Roger is married to Lynette Chandler. Lynette is an Emeritus Professor in the Northern Illinois University's Department of Special Education. She is an author and national authority on Early Childhood Special Education.

Roger Lubeck and Chris Hanson are the authors of:

- *Finding the Right Path: A Guide to Leading and Managing a Title Insurance Company*, 2011.
- *Finding the Right Strategy: How to Grow Income in a Title Insurance Company, 2014*

Roger Lubeck has published ten novels, including:

- *To the Western Border: A Fantasy Adventure*, 2011.
- *Bullseye,* the first Robert Cederberg novel, 2011.
- *Captiva,* the second Robert Cederberg novel, 2012.
- *Port Royal,* the third Robert Cederberg novel, 2013.
- *Key West,* the fourth Robert Cederberg novel, 2015.
- *Overland: Stage from El Paso*, 2016.
- *Ghosts in Horseshoe Canyon*, 2017.
- *On the Half Shell,* 2020
- *PT 777*, 2020
- *Buscadero*, 2021
- *Night Raids*, 2021

Roger was the Editor on:

- *The Day Before the End of the World,* by the Journey, 2012
- *Stories from Other Worlds,* by the Writing Journey, 2014.
- *Every Book Counts: The Stories of My Life*, by Samuel C. Chandler, 2015.
- *Voices from the Dark*, by The Writing Journey, 2015.
- *Untold Stories: From the Deep Part of the Well,* by Redwood Writers, 2016.

Roger was an Associate Editor on:

- *Sunset Sunrise.* Ed. Crissi Langwell, by Redwood Writers, 2020.
- *Endeavor.* Ed. Tommie Whitener, by Redwood Writers, 2019.
- *Redemption.* Ed. Robbi Sommers Bryant, by Redwood Writers, 2018.
- *Sonoma: Stories of region and its people.* Ed. Robert Digitale, by Redwood Writers, 2017.
- *Journeys: On the Road & Off the Map,* Ed. Amber Lea Starfire, by Redwood Writers, 2015.
- *Water,* Ed. Jeanne Miller, by Redwood Writers, 2014.

PRESS

IT IS WHAT IT IS PRESS

Roger C. Lubeck, *Night Raids,* Cloverdale, CA, It Is What It Is Press, 2021.

Roger C. Lubeck, *Buscadero,* Cloverdale, CA, It Is What It Is Press, 2021.

Roger C. Lubeck, *PT 777,* Cloverdale, CA, It Is What It Is Press, 2020.

Roger C. Lubeck, *On the Half Shell,* Cloverdale, CA, It Is What It Is Press, 2020.

Roger C. Lubeck, *Ghosts in Horseshoe Canyon,* Cloverdale, CA, It Is What It Is Press, 2017.

Roger C. Lubeck, *Overland: Stage to El Paso,* Cloverdale, CA, It Is What It Is Press, 2016.

Roger C. Lubeck, *Key West,* Cloverdale, CA, It Is What It Is Press, 2015.

Roger C. Lubeck, *Port Royal,* Cloverdale, CA, It Is What It Is Press, 2013.

Roger C. Lubeck, *Captiva,* Cloverdale, CA, It Is What It Is Press, 2012.

Roger C. Lubeck, *Bullseye,* Cloverdale, CA, It Is What It Is Press, 2011.

Roger C. Lubeck, *To the Western Border: A Fantasy Adventure,* Cloverdale, CA, It Is What It Is Press, 2011.

Roger C. Lubeck and Christopher R. Hanson, *Finding the Right Path: A Guide to Leading and Managing a Title Insurance Company*, It Is What It Is Press, 2011.

Christopher R. Hanson and Roger C. Lubeck, *Finding the Right Strategy: How to Grow Income in a Title Insurance Company,* It Is What It Is Press, 2014.

The Journey, *The Day Before the End of the World*, ed. Roger C. Lubeck, Cloverdale, CA, It Is What It Is Press, 2012.

The Writing Journey, *Stories from Other Worlds, ed.* Ana Koulouris and Roger C. Lubeck, Cloverdale, CA, It Is What It Is Press, 2014.

Samuel C. Chandler, *Every Book Counts: The Stories of My Life,* ed. Roger C. Lubeck, Lynette Chandler, Ruth Chandler, Marianne Chandler Paredes, Cloverdale, CA, It Is What It Is Press, 2015.

The Writing Journey, *Voices from the Dark*, ed. Roger C. Lubeck, Phoenix Autumn, Ana Koulouris, Sara Marschand, K. C. Swier, Cloverdale, CA, It Is What It Is Press, 2015.

Colophon

This book was produced using CreateSpace and Kindle Direct
Publishing tools and services.
The typeface is Garamond and Myraid Pro.